IN THE END THEY TOLD THEM
ALL TO GET LOST

Laurence Leduc-Primeau

IN THE END THEY TOLD THEM ALL TO GET LOST

*Translated from the French by
Natalia Hero*

QC FICTION

Revision: Peter McCambridge
Proofreading: David Warriner, Elizabeth West
Book design: Folio infographie
Cover & logo: Maison 1608 by Solisco
Fiction editor: Peter McCambridge

Originally published under the title *À la fin ils ont dit à tout le monde d'aller se rhabiller*

Translation copyright © Natalia Hero

ISBN 978-1-77186-174-8 pbk; 978-1-77186-175-5 epub; 978-1-77186-176-2 pdf; 978-1-77186-177-9 mobi/pocket

Legal Deposit, 2nd quarter 2019
Bibliothèque et Archives nationales du Québec
Library and Archives Canada
Published by QC Fiction
6977, rue Lacroix
Montréal, Québec H4E 2V4
Telephone: 514 808-8504

QC@QCfiction.com
www.QCfiction.com

QC Fiction is an imprint of Baraka Books.

Printed and bound in Québec

Trade Distribution & Returns
Canada and the United States
Independent Publishers Group
1-800-888-4741
orders@ipgbook.com

We acknowledge the financial support for translation and promotion of the Société de développement des entreprises culturelles (SODEC), the Government of Québec tax credit for book publishing administered by SODEC, the Government of Canada, and the Canada Council for the Arts.

Société de développement des entreprises culturelles
Québec

Canada

Conseil des Arts du Canada   Canada Council for the Arts

I'VE BEEN STARING at you for a week, Betty. Betty the stain. Dirty and alone. I didn't think I'd give you a name when I first got here. A brown stain, on a yellowed wall, in a dirty room. Doesn't deserve a proper noun. But you've started moving. You almost move more than I do. You need a sharp eye to notice; I watch you all day long. You must be alive. I've decided to call you Betty. Traced you with a felt marker, outlined in black, cast in a mold. Now you'll stop moving. You'll stay close to me.

I see you, you know. Don't act all innocent. None of that "innocent until proven guilty" business, that's over now. Done. Understand?

The bed is lumpy. The mattress eroded by its springs. When I stretch out, I can touch all four walls at once. Filthy. There's nothing else I can say about this room. Even if I take a closer look.

Okay, nothing to say, that's not true. There's always something left to say. The ceiling is warped over the foot of the bed. That's something. Warped by humidity. Warped by pus. Warped by mold. It'll collapse tonight. That's what ceilings do.

A fly as big as a butterfly. It bumps into everything. Makes a noise like a radiator on its last legs. Hits the wall, the ceiling, the other wall, brushes against my left ear, gains altitude, lands on the old worn mirror—then changes its mind. Buzzes this way and that, never still, turns around, back and forth. Then disappears from my field of vision.

Silence. It seems to have stopped, finally.

The noise comes back, the bug flies a hair's breadth away from my nose, charges at full speed toward the light and starts turning around it in concentric circles. Doesn't go anywhere near the window, not even for a second.

You poor little idiot, you can't get out of here.

My room looks like a birdhouse, perched on a balcony. Perfect for birds that've lost their wings.

I get everything mixed up. The sounds become muddled, they're all the same. Emilio on the phone. How do I know it's really him? I don't even know how many of them are out there. I land in this country, I almost collapse in his arms. It's ridiculous, he doesn't know where to stand. Chloé? He stiffens. Um, luggage? I have the address in my hand. That's all I have, a crumpled-up piece of paper with 34 B written on it.

Still timid, he points to the back of the courtyard, lets me pass. Marble on the ground, something that was pretty once. He waits for me to go up, keeps his distance. My feet are tired, the steps are tired. I climb, one foot in front of the other, for what feels like an eternity. Here, he says in English, to the left.

The key he hands me weighs four tons. An old-timey key like in the movies, made for opening treasure chests. I go in. He looks at the state of my clothes and lends me a T-shirt. In it, I'm fifteen.

My bags couldn't bear to follow me any longer. They've fled. Sucked up by conveyor belts toward unknown baggage holds. I should have known this was in store for me. I lay out what I have left on the bed. Nothing.

My things scattered, probably for sale in a market in Beijing. They don't belong with all the other stuff on sale, but who cares? A Chinese lady walks by, picks up my favourite skirt. She doesn't notice the hem that's coming undone. She won't be lazy like me, she'll get it fixed. But she'll get sick of the skirt. Way too fast. For her, it'll be a skirt like any other. She'll never know how much it meant to me.

How did you get here, Betty? Have you noticed there's no view from the window?

My God it's humid. How can you stand it? And that noise. It never stops. Enough to drive you insane. The vacuum, the dinners, the babies, the radio, the TV, someone yelling on the phone, the people who use their windows as ashtrays. The cars, the trucks, the buses, the taxis, the horns. This constant vibration that gets inside my skull, penetrates my bones, and never leaves. No wonder they say this town is the therapy capital of the world.

Everyone's crazy here. That's why I came.

You know, Betty, as the plane took off I followed a car with my finger till it disappeared. In some places, there was still snow. I told myself it might be the last time.

I'm so afraid they'll come up and ask me something.

They're laughing. The sound of dishes and sliding chairs. They go from the kitchen to the living room. Six? Ten? Twelve people? The doorbell never stops chiming, voices stream in.

No, that's not it. People come in, the voices talk and the bell rings. Everything in its place. Plates joining their siblings on the table. Glasses clinking. Cheers! Cheers, to health and happiness. Voices that cut each other off and climb on top of each other. They crescendo into bursts, but nothing breaks. One is particularly high-pitched. She laughs like a hyena. What do I know, I've never met a hyena. Another voice answers the high one. Emilio? His is the only name I know.

Sometimes I forget that I've never believed in fairy tales, and I tell myself stories about princesses that I draw on the walls with my toes. It keeps me busy for a while. It's easy, you don't even need to be that tall. Just stretching my legs out, I've got both feet against the wall and I see gardens full of blonde dolls appear, hanging from the elbows of barbarians.

If I pulled out my pencils to draw them, I'd be stuck having to look at them. And admit to myself that they exist.

The dog is barking. Again. What time could it be? What day? It's hot and humid and yet I'm cold.

The paper airplanes I throw out the window land one by one on the ground three storeys below. The little column of air gives them the false impression that there's an outside. My planes pile up, stubbornly refusing to fly. They get cold feet before they've even taken off. They can see there's no way out.

In this room, there's nowhere to be except in bed. Or standing up facing the window. I alternate. Their voices rotate, 'round and 'round, like clockwork.

Finally, they're gone. A small stream of water is leaking downstairs. I should get up to turn it off. Yes. I should.

I hope they left the plug in the sink. And that soon it'll overflow and turn the place into a pool. I'll go play with the little rubber duckie in the empty apartment.

Little duckie under the flooded table, little duckie basking in the sun with the Tupperware, little duckie slowly climbing the wet stairs, step by step. Little duckie playing with the curling iron—while it's plugged in.

Little duckie electrocuted, watching its own brain being fried, its beak opening as if to scream.

Lulled by the sound of the washing machine, I drift in the ocean of my room. I slip far away from here. A deep blue sky. Look at that, Greece. I'm in Greece. Embraced by the salty wind. I'm running on the hot pebbles, burning my feet.

I have only one picture of Greece, a picture from a postcard: white blocks stacked up on the side of a cliff. When I think of Greece, I picture giant sugar cube houses. Ready to jump. And I dream of going there.

Spin cycle now, and my world vibrates more and more powerfully. The washer makes the bed springs squeak. I'm all shaken up. In my mirage, the houses dive into the sea, destroyed by an earthquake. The cubes fizz as they dissolve. I wish they were bright red, in the teal sea. I'd float over the whirlpool. If I sink, all the better.

Everything stops all of a sudden, I'm startled. Steps, too heavy for a girl. Climbing the stairs two at a time, stopping in front of my door.

The seconds last an eternity. I pull the covers over my head. In Greece, the landscape might be devastated but white clothes stay hung on long clotheslines. The shore invaded by flags with no countries. And I walk around with messy hair. Alone. I hear no one. They don't know I'm there.

Emilio pokes his curly-haired head through the door. Says something to me. Eh? He repeats it. Still don't catch it. A walk. Want to come, Chloé?

He must think I'm depressed. What do they think of me? The weirdo upstairs. When's she finally gonna come out? A little later, he comes back with a tub of ice cream.

Emilio has a gentle face. I hate myself for being incapable of anything.

You've got to eat, sometimes. But also sleep. Especially sleep. I forget faces, little by little. But the corner of the wall that I stared at for too long and the folds of the pillowcase have been imprinted, engraved, and they keep coming back to haunt me even though I've wandered far away.

It's the pictures that are the hardest to shake. They linger, flaccid, sticking to my skin. I rip them off but their pieces come together again, rebuild themselves. The slightest little nothing brings them all back.

Smells are just as insidious. You have to go where life doesn't smell like the thing you're trying to forget.

People in the street steer clear of me. They're scared of my face. If only I could laugh.

I'm walking, Betty. So I can say that I'm breathing their air. Don't take it the wrong way. Even when I'm outside, I'm still with you. I walk around the block like a tourist, enthralled with the cracks in the sidewalk. It's windy. Plastic bags fly into my ankles and hook onto my legs. Afraid, I run back inside.

When I stick my head out my window, I can see the neighbours through theirs. The woman stops to fix her hair. The same loose strand, always. We're both watching each other, pretending we can't see one another.

This is the moment I wait for. My favourite distraction.

I wait, my neck strained, for her to turn up. Then she appears and pretends I don't exist. Looks through me and fixes her hair with one swift motion that's almost tragic. Soon, she'll board up her window so she can stop pretending.

I try to imagine them, their life on the other side of that window. Their apartment must be like mine, but inverted. When they set the table, they don't know where to put the little spoons either. They end up throwing everything in a pile in the middle.

I wish I had a fat lady as a neighbour, who spends her days on the phone in her underwear, wearing a pink kerchief on her head. On Sundays, her children and grandchildren would invade the apartment and she'd serve them spaghetti and meatballs, or the local equivalent. Before leaving, they'd all sing the national anthem together.

The morning kicks off with the sound of the coffee maker and hurried footsteps shuffling toward the bathroom. The water from the faucet, the water from the toilet, and then, finally, the shower. Sometimes the steps cross paths and talk to each other. But generally, there are three waves of distinct footsteps. One sometime between 8 and 10, followed by a second, just after the first steps have left, and then a third, much later.

I wait till everything's been quiet for at least fifteen minutes before heading out. I carefully place my feet onto the stairs to make as little noise as possible. Some days, I go out between the second and third waves; some days, after that.

Adriana hands me a pile of clothes without asking what I think of them. I timidly thank her. Adriana is the other girl. Well, *the* girl. She has big black eyes that sparkle. She makes people laugh, she's from Barcelona. If I'd met her at any other time in my life, I'd be cracking up constantly. Every time I see her, her nails are painted a different colour. Sometimes she even alternates between fingers. That's what I notice, the colour of her nail polish.

I met her while she was making herself a coffee. She handed me a cup, salmon-pink nails, started giggling when she saw me: I was still wearing Emilio's T-shirt.

When the other roommates talk to me, on the rare occasions they talk to me, I never know when to cut them off. They talk too fast. And I look at them with my eyebrows raised and tell myself I have to catch one word, just one. The worst will be behind you. But words have a mind of their own. They resist, they escape. They refuse to build bridges but instead weave threads, more bars for my cage.

But I've taken lessons. I thought I knew something, at least.

Every now and then, the vacuum knocks against my door. The impact makes the wood shake and the motor roar even louder. I try to tune the noise out. But it's impossible. It does all it can to get to me. A pillow over my head does nothing.

What a strange idea to have a cleaning lady. I hate that noise. Vrooooom! When the door opens, the noise bursts in, enough to make my eardrums explode.

¡Ay! ¡Oh! ¡Lo siento! And a whole series of words I don't understand. Me llamo Luz. That part I get. I push the pillow against my head. But her words still reach my ears. At this hour, I should be up and about. That's what she told herself.

As a kid, I slept in a single bed with a shabby mattress just like this one. The springs would squeak every time I moved.

I remember I often counted the chimes of the church bell across the street so I'd know how many hours I'd managed not to sleep. I fought off the slumber that tried to slide its way under my eyelids. But some hours seemed longer than others. I suspected that the priest had fallen asleep and lost the bet he didn't know he'd made.

The priest, fallible. Me, I counted the bells, and resisted sleep.

I learned much later that the bells had been automated since before I was born.

Three steps between us that I don't dare take. The dog'll never let me go downstairs. Should I jump over it? Its barking could wake the dead. I bet it knows how to fly. And once I'm on the same floor as it, I don't hold out much hope that I'll make it out alive. No te preocupes, it's because he likes you. Ah! Hadn't realized Emilio was in the kitchen. Did I understand what he said?

The dog never goes out. Except on the balcony, its open-air litter box. That's on a good day, the days when someone's gotten up early enough to open the door for it. But most days, it settles for the foot of the stairs that lead up to my cage. Half-asleep, I've just stepped in some.

It sits there, with its innocent little face, pretending to be nice for once.

Betty, you've moved again. I told you to stop. Why don't you listen to me? I talk to you, and you don't listen. I thought that you would, at least. Come on, be nice. Don't do anything ever again. You want to abandon me, is that it?

In the span of three hours, Betty, the spider's moved less than you have. I hope that teaches you a lesson. That now you understand. That you won't try to cheat me again.

Have you considered meditation?

The Chinese emperor who was buried with an army of terracotta soldiers must have died of fright, finding himself so alone before eternity. His underlings worked their asses off to sculpt serene, gallant faces, the exact opposite of reality. Carving and grinding till the clay looked human, till the darkness became less cold.

No one dared to point out that an army of clay couldn't save him.

Knock knock. ¿Señorita? I don't need cleaning. Luz comes in to shake something out in the room full of nothing. I don't even have four walls to myself. She talks and talks and talks. I don't listen. She wonders what I'm up to, always in my room. Pobrecita. Me, the poor little thing. How ironic.

Luz comes too often, unlocks the door with this particular sound, wakes me up, lines our shoes up in the entrance because it's neater, finishes up the dishes that are lying around. My room smells like mold, both before and after she comes.

There are two spiders now, Betty. Are you feeling the pressure?

I open my bedroom door and see them all below. They don't realize I'm watching. The funniest one is Matías. He lives here too. "Lives." He's barely ever here. I always wonder if there's life behind his closed door. I've watched him a few times. It seems like he doesn't know I exist, or he forgets. When the others aren't here, he chain-smokes and talks to himself while he reads the paper. Today he's pacing back and forth between the kitchen and dining room, naked, reciting something like he's trying to memorize a script. The dog follows him along, scraping its little claws against the floor.

I approach, hesitant. Emilio barely lifts an eyebrow, still half-asleep. He must be wondering why I've come out, all of a sudden. He lives in the living room, on the couch at all hours.

I should have eaten in the kitchen. Now I have to start some kind of conversation. I have nothing to say. I'm just sitting there with my bowl of cereal. I don't have the words. He's going to think I came to get something. Or that I've gotten lost. I'd look even weirder if I turned back without saying a word.

The beast is at the bottom of the stairs, waiting to jump me. It growls, drool dripping from the side of its mouth. It stands on its hind legs, jumps around all over the place. I scream, tell it to get lost and wave my arms around. But this dog only speaks Spanish, and not very well at that. Often, I stay upstairs just so I don't have to deal with it. It doesn't belong to anyone. It doesn't have a name. Shut up, dog. Chill out.

¡Cállate! It listens to Emilio. It's afraid of him. Me, not so much.

Emilio shows up with eggs wrapped in kraft paper. I point at the eggs; he doesn't understand. ¿Dónde, um. ¿Dónde comprar? He smiles and finishes my thought: ¿Huevos frescos?

He starts talking. Realizes it's no use, half of it goes over my head. Scribbles a map on a sheet of paper, full of arrows and street names. He writes Mercado at the corner of two streets I don't know. I've never ventured out that far.

I wander in circles, I can't find it. Mercado. Are we talking about the same thing? I go around the block again. A woman steps out of what looks like a ramshackle warehouse with a bag of vegetables. Seems weird to hide a market like that. I go inside. Live chickens, dead pigs. Their eyes fixed on me. I keep going. Bags being weighed and exchanged. How do they understand each other? Last time your strawberries were no good, try to pull that with me again and I'm taking my business elsewhere. And your wife?

I want cucumbers. Zanahoria? Concumbre? I think they're asking me how many. Dos. I signal with my hand at the same to be sure. She fills a bag, weighs it, adds more. What is she doing? Two, I said two! The scale says two kilos. I give up. I pay her.

In the middle of the market, old people sit at a café. They comment on the horse races on TV as they sip their espressos. The first nods his head and makes little noises with his mouth. Tut tut. The other keeps going no, no, no—not raising his voice, but sounding exasperated. The first puts his head in his hands, gets frustrated. They're insulting each other now, maybe. The second slams a bill down on the counter. ¡Paco! A third, who was hanging around nearby, grabs a stool, steps between the first two. And things get heated. No es eso. ¡Escuchame! They're not watching the horses anymore, they could be talking about anything. A woman wearing heavy makeup, with a tiny dog, stands in the corner, not talking to anyone. Just looks at her dog. That looks like a rat.

The bartender has seen worse. He's not interested in the witch, or the rat-dog, or the blasé old gamblers. He spins a bottle opener between his fingers, focused on the screen, takes forever to come see me.

He doesn't know this is my first smile.

I'm jotting down words, phrases, and expressions that I hear in this big notebook I just bought. The ones I hear, that I repeat to myself, that I've already caught and that I'll forget. But there are words that bounce off of me, that refuse to enter my brain. Gracioso. Gra-cio-so. Graaaaaaaa-cioooooooo-soooooo. Dame un traigo. Trago? Traguo?

When Adriana talks on the phone, she parks herself on the couch with her feet up on the table, the phone wedged between her shoulder and ear. She floods whoever she's talking to with a cascade of words as she paints her nails. This ride could easily last an hour. She giggles. Wriggles about so much that the person she's talking to can probably feel it on the other end. Her voice like a roller coaster scattered with laughter. After her nails, she fixes her hair. And by the time she's ready, it's dark out.

At the grocery store, I stand for a long time in front of the wall of names I don't understand. Too many bottles, too many choices. I can't decide, I pick up the first thing that comes to hand. We're celebrating Emilio's birthday tonight. The big 3-0.

I hide in the corner, between the table and the wall. If I'd wanted to disappear completely, I couldn't have done a better job. Matías is chatting with people at the other end of the living room. From where I'm standing, it looks like he's getting worked up over just about everything. But that's just the impression I get from a distance. He probably doesn't even know I'm his new roommate.

The apartment's full of people. Everyone interrupting each other, yelling, brushing up against me without noticing I'm there. I eat some olives.

You're not supposed to talk with your mouth full. Emilio introduces me to Alberto, Claudia, and Beatriz, who leave me right away. Then he leaves me too. These olives are great, I say to no one.

Alberto and Beatriz start arguing across the room. Are they a couple? Were they a couple? They burst out laughing. I polish off the olives.

Cubes of cheese are piled up next to the empty bowl. Ham cubes, too. Everything in cubes, like in space. An aspiring suitor appears at my side. Will he save me?

In slow and simple Spanish, he sums up what's happening for me. A certified interpreter from normal Spanish to simpleton Spanish. His hair is greasy. La chica allá, la colorada, sí. Es la ex de Emilio. Una locura. He waits for an answer, a signal from me to go on. What does he want me to say? She's crazy, I get it. The ex is crazy.

I'm struck by these insane urges to suck off a gun barrel.

Whose finger is on the trigger? Jude Law's.

You know what, Betty? I'm not getting up today.

No one's explained Luz's schedule to me. The others always make sure they're out when she comes. It's only with the sound of the front door opening, that specific noise her keys make in the lock, that I know it's a cleaning day. I grind my teeth. I brace myself for the worst.

Sometimes, I watch her work. I go down to the kitchen, and I tell myself that I am, that we are, exploiters. And that watching her is taking part in that exploitation. She turns to me, shoots me a maternal smile. Impervious to my victimization attempts. Protecting me, rather, from this cruel world. Me, the poor child who doesn't understand a thing. ¿Un té? I can't even muster a thank you.

I've had enough. My head is exploding. Give me a hammer, something.

The marble is colder than the rest. Harder, too. With my hair undone, starfished out on the floor, I don't care. I thought there was nothing here. I didn't look properly. A can rusting on some branches and a little pile of leaves. I wonder how they got there. Brought by the birds, I imagine. Letting their piles of shit fall as they fly by, that dries all around me, in matching tones on the old marble. I think of all the piles of shit that I'm not seeing.

Any curious onlookers watching from their windows must be eating this up. Too rare a spectacle in this courtyard that's usually empty: this intruder sprawled out on the ground with her hair full of cat piss. Normally, in these indoor courtyards, you should be wearing your best clothes. Or what's left of them.

From here, I can see the sky—no birds. I can see the stone arches over the windows, all the same, all in a row. Something medieval about their style. Or antiquated, rather. I live in a roman amphitheatre. In a cheap imitation of a roman amphitheatre. What luxury.

The gladiators will come through the door to fight in the arena. Come on, come get me. Release your horses, wave your clubs, your metal skirts. Show no mercy. Put on a show for everyone watching, with dried-up spit on your clothes, fight for me. Come on in, gentlemen. Show me the sacrifices you're prepared to make. Gladiators to the core. And me at the end of the sword. How far will you go?

I want to see blood. In my honour.

Diesel makes me think of a communist state.

Sometimes I can't see at all. The bus in front of mine spits long streaks of black smoke that enters through the open windows and envelops the passengers. My nails are always black with pollution, I can never get them clean. It's a smell that sticks to the city, to the skin. That condemns us.

Car horns blare and the bus almost flips over. A horse and buggy cut us off. I grip my seat with both hands, stuck between rows of strangers. The bus crosses an avenue built for military parades.

I'd rather tell myself that it's for a queen, a majestic royal procession. From times when having a horse was a sign of wealth. The whole city would follow and throw confetti. Or flowers. Flowers are better.

A dead-end street. I tell myself that there have been blazing infernos, ambushes, deaths over there. And a child sitting on a pile of debris, holding a flag. No. He's in another story. Many try to escape. The smoke suffocates them. Carnage. Another sharp turn, I fall onto a new neighbour. Perdón. No reaction.

Anyway, I'm just a foreigner.

Sometimes, when the apartment's empty, I'll go into the kitchen. A stove, a fridge, counters, shelves. I open doors and find plates, rice, boxes of cookies. It looks like a normal kitchen. But all the things in there feel threatening, they kick me out.

There are moments, sometimes even whole minutes, when I can understand without having to translate. It's sort of subconscious. Their lips will move, they'll make sounds and, in my head, words will arrive and form images that make connections. But if I stop to try to make sense of the mechanism, I lose everything. Their sounds become abstract noises again and line my brain with tones and accents that pile up, waiting to be put to use.

The notebook is starting to fill up with words I'm afraid I'll forget. Or the common words that have nothing to do with anything. Sábana, bolsa, grifo, medias. But I rarely read over the first few pages. I guess deep down I do know the older words.

Hunched over a stack of paper, Emilio briefly waves his hand to let me know not to disturb him. The TV's still on, but he's turned the sound off. The more focused he is, the closer his ear moves to his shoulder.

What is he working on that makes him twist his neck up like this?

He takes a sip of the cold coffee on the table next to him. It's probably been there since yesterday. The carafe glued to layer upon layer of sticky circles. Never a full circle, more like three quarters of one. He scribbles all over a page, draws some arrows on it, throws it away, picks it up again.

I used to have a brain. There was a time when I ripped my hair out over things. As I watch him, I realize I've forgotten how to do it. The attention span of a goldfish is eight seconds.

One of these days, I really need to find something to do.

I go out and buy one apple and two celery stalks. I add them to the fridge next to my pitiful yogurt and little chunk of cheese, all alone among the other vegetables. Alone up against everyone else's vegetables.

The people in the cafe are so beautiful and chic. I sit and order tea and little almond cupcakes that are served in porcelain dishes. The garden smells like lily of the valley, vines crawl up the walls, you'd think I was in a rich fancy country. Tables surrounded by wrought iron chairs painted in all these different pastel colours. Colours that clash just enough for me to tell myself that they picked them on purpose to look like candy.

I pull out a notebook that I don't write in. I'm too busy letting myself float. The only detail that stops me from getting carried away with the dreamy ambiance of this garden is the smell. Lilies are my grandmother. The times I spent at her house climbing trees, swinging, building myself little forts, setting traps all over the yard. Ironically, the smell of lilies always made me sick. It smells too strong. It creeps up your nose.

The garden is populated by couples. Twos, all completely engrossed in being together. Come on baby, open your mouth, here comes the airplane. The spoon stays suspended in the air while the mouth waits, open, stupid, for the hand to feed it. Airplane noises as it waits. The mouthful ends up missing its target, falling to the ground. Little cream cake stain on the lawn.

All that's missing's a poodle to complete the perfect picture of successful lovers. They look at the lost bite and laugh. If I were them I'd be ashamed. They start again. Open your mouth wide, darling. Wider. Even wider. What'll they do next, bottle feed each other?

I breathe.

The waitress gives me a strong feeling of déjà-vu. Tall, thin. Her enormous glasses slide down her nose. She pushes them up with her index finger. With this jaded, exasperated, too-cool-for-you look on her face. She's wearing bright pink leggings and a grey low-cut top. Where have I seen her before?

Restless kids run between the tables. Their mother angrily calls them back to order. I give her a sign with my head that I don't care if these kids are acting like kids. She doesn't smile at me.

Putting faces to memories, places, eras, makes me feel like I'm untangling the plot of my life. Like I'm giving breath to the pictures that cross my path. They become more real, more dense.

Gloria. That's her name.

Ya nos vimos, ¿no? She glares at me like I'm an insect, then turns around and leaves.

I have seen her before. I live in a box, I should be able to figure out where I've seen her.

You know Emilio? She drops my fork, apologizes. I live with him. She composes herself. Ah, the Canadian.

I'm fascinated by the speed at which a few magic words take us from the realm of insects to the human world.

When night falls, steel shutters roll down over windows, garage doors, and storefronts. Everything is double-locked. And the streets empty. Taxis, multiplied by darkness, wait by doors to shuttle partygoers from one haunt to the next. They say this city is all about going out. I think it's all about staying in, about secured interiors sheltered from the demons roaming the streets.

In a city where everyone's crazy, clearly there are more ghosts hanging around.

Señorita, ayúdeme. It isn't a question. The old lady orders me to take her bags. Yes, you, right now. She's gotta be like a hundred years old. Her hand is limp, clammy. I help her up the stairs. In her other hand, she holds a cane.

As soon as she gets the chance, she starts whacking my ankles with it. Hey! With no explanation. Faster? Slower? Come on, she calls to me, her workhorse. And cracks her whip. Her cane calibrated to sting just enough to get me going. Vicious old hag. Maybe she'll spend days after this recalling her triumph. Maybe she reels in a different prey every time, and really she's a professional sprinter. Her door moves further and further from sight, almost disappears from my field of vision, más allá, más allá. That'll teach me to want to be nice.

Behind some furniture in the living room, I find some photo booth pictures. Emilio and Matías and a girl I don't know striking silly poses, dressing up, frowning, hugging and kissing.

These pictures always look like they're witnesses to the perfect summer day. The kind of moment that we'll forever regret having missed out on. Friends or lovers, crammed into a booth with the curtain drawn, taking the time to create a memory they'll be able to keep, that marks an era.

In high school, you had to collect them, and show them off. Whose faces did you manage to shove yours between? I remember ordinary moments that we tried to transform into extraordinary memories. I've always been jealous of pictures I'm not in.

The beast found a bone. It runs through my legs, head first into the wall because it's too dumb to stop in time. It picks it up again, growls, barks, follows me everywhere drooling, making weird noises as it gnaws on it. It's probably telling itself a story where it's the hero. It's found the Bone. El Bone. And it won't come back down to earth as long as there's some of it left. Stupid fucking dog, let me go! What idiot let this thing into the apartment? One of these days I'm gonna grind it up into sausages.

Emilio in the kitchen, wearing an apron. Dirty dishes piled up all around him. Luz will be happy tomorrow. I didn't know you could cook. If I could cook! I taught the Italians how to make pizza. Adriana's in a good mood. Emilio's acting all flirty. Even Matías is here. I decide to stay. I have to start living a little.

Emilio's an actor. He writes plays and teaches theatre classes.

I have a drink with Adriana while the men handle the cooking. Her nails are coral. Yesterday she brought home a boy I didn't catch a glimpse of. Always someone new.

Matías arrives with an animal fresh from the oven, surrounded by roasted garlic. The famous pizza will have to wait till another time. I kind of wonder if we're celebrating something. The dog jumps up and down like it's possessed and tries to climb up onto the table. It doesn't realize how ugly it is.

Glasses emptied and filled. The evening stretches on. What do you think of our country? Why exactly did you come here? Don't you get bored, holed up at home? What do you do in your room?

I sketch doubtful answers and blame my bad Spanish. I want the questions to stop. The conversation drifts to Matías's chaotic love life. A lot of it goes over my head. Like a switch has been flipped, and I can't hear anymore. The words become insignificant buzzes.

And then, all of a sudden, we're in party mode.

Emilio's banging on a pan. Matías joins in with glasses and forks. Adriana too, with a wooden spoon on the radiator. A beautiful sight. They go on like that for a while. I stare, hypnotized. Their rhythm steadies. Emilio comes up to me with a big pot. ¡Dale Chloé! ¡Tocá! Puts it down in my lap.

There's a long moment where I do nothing. Emilio's already gone to get another instrument. I look at the pot. The other two haven't noticed, they're banging on whatever makes noise.

I sit there on the chair, with the pot on my knees. The other three playing a concerto in cast-iron major. I start timidly tapping with the tips of my fingers. I can barely hear the sound I'm making. Louder and louder. Boing – tap – tap – mm – tap. I start to gain a little confidence, and eventually I'm playing in time with the others. I start to forget, a little. Emilio sings, Matías and Adriana too. I start tapping my foot. We get louder and louder. The rhythm accelerates, the noise becomes chaotic. Now more of an amateur ambiance. The boys stand up on their chairs. They're singing themselves hoarse. They start competing to see who can outdo the other. Cocky as roosters.

And, in a flurry of emotion, Emilio falls off. Everyone has a laughing fit. The chair's broken.

Betty, have you ever noticed that time isn't linear? On TV, a woman wearing too much makeup replaces another. Then another. Then another. Her piercing, high-pitched voice doesn't change. Close-up on her tanned face, a look of despair. She hiccups. Sobs that sound half-stuck at the bottom of her throat. Elevator music reminds us of her happier years.

The screen goes black and gives way to a bright, hazy scene. The same face, radiant, on a man's shoulder, alone in the middle of a field, on a plaid picnic blanket. He puts a flower behind her ear. She's smiling, brings a piece of chocolate to her lips. The camera lingers on a passing butterfly, follows it. The lovers leave the frame, and in the distance, hills. The butterfly flies out of frame to the right and the camera stops moving. Stays fixed on the green hills.

Another cut, to the blonde lady drinking vodka straight from the bottle. Zoom in on her running mascara.

If I had guts, even just a little, I'd take all the plates, one by one, and throw them as hard as I could onto the floor.

The fuck are you looking at? Don't look at me like that! Hasn't anyone ever taught you that it's rude to stare? Of course not, you stupid dog, no one's ever taught you anything. Bastard. You just bark, that's it. If you're looking for trouble, you're gonna find it. I lost my earring, okay? That's what's happening here.

I'm looking for my earring. Understand? You're happy to see me on the ground, is that it? Don't get snarky with me. I'm not the one pissing all over the place. Get lost!

Listen, dog, if you lick me, I'm gonna kill you. Got it?

As a kid, I was terrified of other people's distress. Screams would ricochet around, making holes everywhere. They would tear at my ears, stab me in the gut. I'd hide under tables and wait. Convinced that the apocalypse was imminent. I dreamed of being bulletproof.

They'd end up calming down, start looking for me like we were playing a game. When they'd find me, they'd say ah, you're hiding down there again. Are you practicing to become a spy? Come on, come have dinner, that's enough exploring for one day, it'll get cold.

I should have gone into the kitchen with my red raincoat on and told them it was so their screams would slide right off me.

Once, just once, I let my guard down completely and I found myself, confident, blind, my mouth full of I love yous.

Love has always been a dangerous word. A word that only serves as collateral. Do you love me? You don't love me.

So hypocritical. Love doesn't sound true unless it comes with nothing, never, not anymore. Love is tallied, taken back. Sometimes it's rented. But it isn't given.

If you love me, what do you want from me? I'm heartless. I don't love.

Adriana's making out with a new boy in the living room. Her nails blood red. Red like the scar that's still on the inside of my wrist.

That's not true. It isn't red like blood or red like her nails. It's white.

White and smooth. But I still see it as red, as though it hadn't healed at all since that afternoon. The day I squeezed a tourniquet around my arm and opened it with a box cutter. I had this deep conviction that it wouldn't bleed. Blood is for the living.

There's a puddle of water on the floor of the shower. Water filled with everyone's filth that refuses to drain. It laps around my ankles.

Hair from at least three different heads is caught in the drain, along with hair elastics, a bit of leftover soap that hasn't melted yet, a bobby pin. Sticky, slimy, sick. The deeper I dig, the more surprises I find. At the bottom, it starts to look like tar.

I smear two lines of the gunk across my cheeks and look at myself in the mirror. I'm incapable of smiling at myself. Some people pay a fortune for mud baths, when you could get it for free from a shower drain.

With the tar on my face, I climb the steps to my room, leaving behind a wet trail that will drip down through the stairs and onto the floor. Maybe the dog'll slip on it.

Betty the Stain is bored, I'm giving her the same tired lines over and over again without even trying to be coherent. From the wall where she reigns, she tells me she understands. Misery is always universal, in a way, she says. Same same but different.

I recognize the voices of every couple arguing in the building. Five of them, by my count. Some scream at each other in the morning, others at night. Josefina screams louder than all the rest.

He never answers her. I think she's screaming at the wall. Apparently they have ears. That's what she's doing, taunting the walls' ears. Just once, someone answered her, Josefina, ¡cállate! Loud enough to shut her up, loud enough to shut up all the sounds of the night.

And that's how I found out her name.

I barely recognize myself. Perched on these glittery heels, wrapped up in a blue dress that's way too asymmetrical. Adriana has disguised me as a girl.

The club is packed. They're all drooling over my roommate. I imagine they're not buying my get-up. One of them is lingering near me anyway. He's figured out that he's fifth in line for Adriana and there's no use trying—he won't be going home with her. He's not bad looking.

The game of seduction is universal. Since the music is too loud for us to hear each other, we rely on body language. The gazes. The forwardness. The rapport we strike up, or don't. The despair, too. The desire not to end up alone at the end of the night. I look the guy up and down. Yes, no, maybe.

Yeses are dangerous. They could rip my heart out without even realizing it. That's what they're after, really. One look from me, a desperate girl who's all over them, so they can feel like they exist. My big green eyes give them life, and help them keep up this game, over and over again, of trying to impress me. The Nos won't be spending the night with me. No chance. I won't even look at them, too bad. The Maybes, it depends. Depends on them, depends on me. Depends on the night, and what I'm prepared to sacrifice to let myself be liked a little. Some nights, I need to believe it. I tell myself it's all good fun, because I never get to have fun anymore. I drink too much. Sometimes I manage to convince myself that I can't help it. That's what I keep saying to whoever will listen, anyway. I tell them whatever I need to, to stop myself from getting tripped up by the consequences. They play along with it, they encourage me. Tomorrow, I'll tell the guy who took me home, I'll say, Did you believe it? He'll answer No, of course not. We'll laugh like children and tell people about that night like it's a story that happened to someone else.

He buys me a drink. I down it in one gulp. Eventually, I forget I'm his second choice.

He puts his hand around my waist, whispers in my ear. He tugs gently at my hair, draws circles around my earrings with his fingers, lets them dangle. He calls me guapa, kisses my neck, gets me to drink some more. He follows a script he's rehearsed so many times before he almost feels it.

He's an actor. They're all actors in this country.

Another drink. I hope he takes me for a foreign babe he can show off, I hope he finds me exotic. No matter how many times I tell myself that anyone will do, I'm frozen to the spot.

I kiss him, and nothing. I remember a time when lips brushing against my neck would have sent electric shocks flying from head to toe. Anyone's lips.

I feel the wind on my bare shoulders. I wander aimlessly. Till sunrise. Down to the landfill river.

There's a pack of eight, maybe ten dogs stalking me. A howl at the moon reminds me that stray dogs are almost wolves. Just the thought of their claws scraping against the pavement, sharpening, chills me to the bone.

They all have rabies, for sure, they're feral. I'm not sure why, but I grip my girly little dress, all frail between the parked pickup trucks of tattooed sailors who stare as I walk by, the dogs trailing behind me. These stupid heels.

I wonder who'll jump me first; the dogs, or them.

Matías is still up. I'm feeling shy, all of a sudden, just being in the same room as him. He offers me a puff of his cigarette without a word. I think of my life expectancy shrinking before my eyes and accept it. What's a potential number on an abstract scale? The smoke rises up to the ceiling.

Matías would have made a good aristocrat. There's something about his posture and presence that makes you want to admit you've been bested before the games even begin. He turns the page of his newspaper, seems to be reading attentively. Adriana must be off with one of her suitors. Maybe mine found some other girl before the night ended. Probably.

I lean my head on Matías's shoulder and pass my hand through the cloud of escaping smoke. It breaks up the smoke but leaves no trace.

When I was little, in the spring, I'd build dams for little streams. The water would flow along the sidewalk and I'd block its path to the sewer drain. With slush, whatever was left of the snow, bits of wood. When the water pressure got too strong, my dam would break up into tiny pieces. And the water would pick up speed again, and happily work its way back to the hole.

What I liked most of all was imagining that the water, the slush, and the branches had a will of their own. That I was barely doing anything at all. Just helping things along.

I think I might be autistic. Establishing a real, deep, sincere connection is impossible. I watch these people moving around in front of me, living. I try to behave like them. I'm not good at anything but copying, imitating. Repeating until my brain takes note and catches on. When in doubt, I abstain completely. They take me for a quiet girl, timid and reserved.

Emilio emerges. ¿Venís? Gracias, pero no. He shrugs and smiles. Leaves with a spring in his step.

Querida, what is it you want? I've got everything you need. Barato, barato. I go well out of my way to shake off the street vendors. Unrolled, the pareo looks like a colourful island on the ground that dissolves into dust when I touch it. It looks like sand. Like in westerns, the sand flying up excitedly under the feet of the new cowboy in town that the director loves to show in a dramatic close-up.

People, everywhere. And their eyes. As long as I don't make eye contact.

The earth, and my hands in it. A little cloud of dirt. Greyish brown. Dirt or sand, same thing. Dried up and crumbled. I sprinkle it, it flies off in the wind. Not looking at anything else. The pareo, the ground, the dirt. Scratching, ripping, throwing. Focusing on these simple, repetitive movements.

A baby bird slowly moves forward, trips. His little feet are so frail, there are so many obstacles. He gets up, keeps going, falls. Gets back up and tries again. He's going to die soon, unless someone takes care of him. He's too little, way too little.

I'm mesmerized by his movements, the way I sometimes get lost staring at flames. Keep going, little abandoned bird. Come on. Did you fall from your nest? Come here, I can take care of you. I'll make a little spot for you on the windowsill. Comfortable. Not too far from Betty. I could tell you stories, you could sing to me. It would be so nice. I'd help you heal.

Then suddenly, he turns to face me. He's missing an eye. Ew! What a freak.

Get out of here! Don't touch me.

Emilio is having a coffee. Matías too.

There are flies, always. Big ones, small ones. I kill some, they multiply. I think of buying frogs and spiders, leaving them in the kitchen and in my bedroom. It would be a nice change.

They must have pet stores here. How do you say frog? Frog-os? Not sure that works. Maybe Emilio knows where I can find some. He's the kind of guy who wouldn't notice if all the furniture disappeared. What would he care about a frog or two in the mix? Adriana, on the other hand, I'm not so sure about.

¡AHHHHH! ¡Joder, tío, qué es esta mierda!

It's my new frog! You don't like him?

They didn't get up this morning. Three closed doors, half-lit by the afternoon sun. A lot of shoes by the door. I trip over them on my way out.

At the café, the waiter tells me I have to order something more substantial than water if I want to stay. I roll the slice of lemon around the rim of my glass, ignoring him. A man who bears a strange resemblance to the one from the bar the other night crosses the street. I can't help but follow him with my gaze. The one who was pulling on my earrings. Hair just like his, something about his attitude.

Was he tall? It was dark.

I'm not even sure I'd be able to recognize him. Maybe my skin would remember his scent.

Adriana has been baking big batches of cookies since she got up. When they're done she
files them away in metal boxes, with wax paper
between layers. Puts sprinkles on top. She
decided she's getting into the cookie-selling
business. Everyone else does it, so why not? The
smell reminds me that I'm hungry.

Her nails are turquoise. She doesn't pay
attention to me. I reheat my coffee. I open the
fridge: nothing.

Dare I steal Emilio's yogurt?

Marry me, guapa. I've been in love since the moment I laid eyes on you. Don't make me suffer like this. Come back, my love! You're killing me! Say something!

A man is following me down the street, blowing kisses. Hovering around me, trying to take my hand. A moist spot where I pull mine away. Can't think about it or I'll crack. I put my head down and bite the insides of my cheeks. I can't let him know that his little game almost brightened my day. I bite down harder.

I should say yes one day. Let's get married. The guy would be speechless. A short-lived victory; he'd probably say yes.

How do the other girls manage not to laugh?

Luz is up to her elbows in our dishes. The others are gone, obviously. ¿Te vas a quedar mucho por acá? And she tells me about the nearby cathedral I should visit. The relics, the heart, or the arm of some martyr saint who suffered more than any other. The Lord intervened, it was a miracle, a real one. Maybe they even saw the Virgin Mary there. The cathedral has been famous ever since. Luz gesticulates a lot with her arms, shows me the medallion she wears around her neck. She squeezes my wrist, ¿Chloé, vas a ir? What I gather, mostly, is that inside you can barely hear the sounds of the street.

At the grocery store, the cashier is flirting with the lady who lives next door. He asks how her family is. Puts a handful of candy in her hand, for the little one. Last time, a watermelon appeared in her bag. A long wink. To me, he gives the worst vegetables. Barely deigns to serve me.

From the alley, I can still see her. A stray strand of her hair falls onto her neck. She half-heartedly puts it back into place, then lets her hand casually slide onto the cashier's.

I think I'm losing weight.

Emilio's two bearded friends chain-smoke hand-rolled cigarettes with no filters, filling a seashell-shaped ashtray. They've come to watch auteur films and pretend they're Che. So what? Do you find it funny? Adriana's brought her nail polish, just in case. I join them on the too-soft couch.

Emilio watches a new film every day. Preferably something old or independent, from a director who doesn't make it to Cannes or Sundance, but rather festivals like Motovun, or other ones from cities with names I can't pronounce.

He often falls asleep during the movies. Sometimes he'll spend two or three days awake, then sleep for 24 hours, in the living room. But today, with his friends, he keeps his eyes wide open.

He casually mentions that they're looking for someone to work the front desk at his theatre. ¿Te gustaría?

I talk enough now that I can endlessly repeat the same phrases. And I decide that they'll like my cereal box accent.

The overheated room smells like waiting human flesh. I join the pack and sit next to a blonde girl who looks about my age. Her name is Anke. She's German. Second time dancing the old visa waltz. The first time around, she waited five hours just to be told they couldn't accept her birth certificate. Not certified by an official state translator. Please come back with the official documents, miss. Thank you and goodbye. Looking over the papers they've given me, I see that I'll also be needing a police certificate and a copy of my fingerprints.

I look at the people stuffed into the waiting room, with their ears pointed toward the hissing speaker. After a long silence, dos cientos cuarenta y uno, ventanilla B. I barely understand the mumbled, massacred number and already, I know. I know that I'm a future illegal alien.

Anke spends her days wandering around, people-watching, drinking coffee. At least she goes out. She liked the botanical garden. Do you know the Romanof? Obviously not. What do you think of Martinez's last decision? We dive into this zig-zaggy conversation, making ridiculous, laboured efforts not to speak English. She studied cultural management, she's always dreamed of coming here. When she asks where I'm

87

from, I say Canadá without thinking. I regret it immediately. I should have said Quebec, maybe she would have thought it was some distant land, somewhere near Uzbekistan.

My ice cream is slowly melting, dripping down my fingers. A peach-caramel stream, another one that's chocolate. I lick up the liquid spill. Around the cone, down the back of my arm.

Everyone's obsessed with ice cream in this country.

That's one thing they really get. Given the number of ice cream parlours here, and the number of crazy people, I can conclude that ice cream is no cure for madness. Might madness be proportional to the number of ice cream parlours per square inch? Warrants further investigation.

Saturday afternoons, at exactly 2:30 p.m., the neighbour upstairs blasts the *Goldberg Variations*. The same piece, at the same time, every single week. I hear the footsteps go into the living room, then stop when he presses Play. Four steps. Then nothing. The music invades my apartment. And I picture him on a faded green suede recliner. I try to follow his steps and stand right underneath his feet. Then I sit down too, cross-legged on the floor, and close my eyes.

From time to time, the wind blows little red flowers onto the floor, and the bed. They come from the plant I bought myself. It's romantic, these little polka dots everywhere. I enter a palace of petals, scattered under my feet by an imaginary lover.

Emilio catches me on his way out to teach a class. Come, he says. You can ask about the job. He told them about me. They said they'd have to see. Which, here, means nothing.

I'm curious to see where he works, and where I might work, so I follow him. I wasn't expecting an industrial bunker. The ceilings are incredibly high. Most of the inside walls are concrete. All the dust makes it look like spotlights are cutting through the air with a knife. The paintings hanging crooked all over the walls add to the ambiance. The contrast is remarkable.

Emilio shows me around the auditorium and backstage. It's taboo for me to be invading this sanctuary reserved for seasoned pros. Only people who aren't afraid of their own shadow are supposed to be behind these walls.

The dressing room looks like any other room, and yet, I'm hyper-aware that I'm in a *dressing room*, where actors get ready to perform on stage. You have to carry yourself differently, breathe without disturbing the air.

I'm scared to move. Actors have this amazing ability to slide into someone else's skin. To play, to expose themselves, and to believe in it. They become this other person for the duration of the play, then go back to who they really are, without losing themselves along the way.

It sticks to their skin, it overflows. I wish I was like them. I trip over my words. When they ask what I'm doing with my life, I don't know what to say. Nothing. Nothing as small or as big as what you're doing. I don't do anything.

That guy's the boss. *The boss*, it feels weird to call him that. He isn't much older than me. He talks really loud, which makes the hairs of his mustache tremble. Tied to a bed, dressed up like a wrestler straight out of a carnival, he must cry out under the whip of dominatrixes in leather corsets.

The more he talks, the more I see the whip leave marks on his ass with hard, dry slaps. I hear his supplicant cries, alternating between Mercy and Again. He looks me up and down. His mustache quivering above his lips. I pull out my arsenal of smiles. He ends up saying Alright, you start Saturday. He feels the need to add that if it doesn't work out, we're not keeping you. I'm mesmerized by his mustache hairs.

When I was 6, I didn't dance. No ballet recitals, no pink tutus. I played rugby with my Playmobil. Dancing was for the weak. I impulsively push open the door of this dance studio that advertises Talleres de danza contemporánea, ¡Ingresa ahora! The colour, maybe? I'm not dressed for movement, but I don't look totally out of place either. I set my bag down in the room, still riding this strange high. But as soon as I drop it, I freeze. Fifteen or so girls of all ages say hi to each other.

I start to beat a strategic retreat, but then the instructor crosses the room and aims right for me. Please don't come talk to me. I answer primera vez before I even hear her question. She grabs my shoulders and leads me to the middle of the pack, making my escape even more difficult. Confronted by my silence, she relents. Anyway, the class is starting. For a warmup, improvisational dancing around the room. That's what I gather, anyway. I try to melt into the background. I pretend I'm a tree, a kangaroo, a kite, someone who's paralyzed in one leg. They all throw themselves onto the floor at once. I'm the only one left standing, so I get down, too. No doubt just to embarrass me, they all jump back up at once. My wrist hurts, I keep going. I'm not sure if it's a choreography they've all rehearsed before or some intuitive fusion with the dancing gods.

She catches me before I can manage to disappear. Carmen. You'll be back, she says.

Naming things, or people, sort of makes them belong to me. The more I stick words onto the things that surround me, the more their outline becomes clear to me. I call Anke-my-New-German-Friend. The Raval, tonight at 11?

It's funny, I do manage to forget, sometimes. It's always the stupidest, tiniest little thing that brings everything flooding back.

I throw a paper airplane out the open window. It nosedives and falls to the ground. Crumpled up with all the others.

On TV, a documentary about moose, in Sweden or Norway, that kill drivers. And the poor rangers that have to put them down. Footage of elk getting too close to cities, others that cross the street where they shouldn't. I can't seem to empathize. I can't seem to inflate my heart with sadness, the way I should, for these poor innocent beasts being slaughtered by poor innocent men. I force myself to watch, like self-flagellating with despair, to punish myself for existing.

I examine their pots, their spices. I try to do the same and fail. They aren't mine. There's something missing. Always something missing. How did I use to do this? I try to cheer myself on, tell myself that today, maybe, I'll do a proper grocery run and cook myself a real meal. But there's never anything there. I go up and down the aisles, no cheese, no bread. I leave empty-handed and dejected.

Boil some water. More pasta à la nothing.

How do flies fuck? Seriously, how is it possible? Don't flies only have asses?

Matías doesn't give a shit about my moods. He doesn't look at me like I need to be entertained, kept busy. Not like you, Betty. Reminding me once again that if you were me, you'd be doing just fine. Other people's problems always seem so simple. Even a stain knows that.

The rubber duck that was in the bathroom is gone. It's flown away to a beautiful, promising, distant land. If you'd asked me, little duckie, I'd have told you that's not the best move. It's like Luz's daughter. She collapsed in my arms when she told me about her, no one knows where she's ended up.

In memoriam del ducko, I light some candles and take a bath with tons of bubbles. The tub isn't big enough for my shoulders and knees to be in the water at once, so I alternate. I add more water just to see the steam escape into the air, put my feet under the boiling stream coming from the faucet, leave them there till they're raw. And then do it all over again.

Adriana has evaporated. I shoot a few smiles at the strangers at the vernissage as I hesitantly wander through the exhibit. I've lost my only pillar. Superimposed filters at weird angles give the pictures on the walls a mystical aura. The photographer named his exhibit "Improbable Spaces: Dreamy Cities and Veiled Nightmares." I recognize some of the places in the pictures. The abandoned buildings, the port, the factory near the river that blows purple smoke. Even my neighbourhood market, floating in the middle of red fabric.

I stop in front of a black and white one. A chair in the middle of an industrial wasteland. I feel naked. The photographer is standing next to me. That one's my favourite too, he says.

We stand there suspended, him and I, contemplating, maybe the same things. The picture is infinite. Full of a void that scratches away from the inside, that sucks me in and, strangely, soothes me.

Later, at the bar, the photographer comes up to me. He tells me that he just got back from Iraq. And that after illegally crossing the border, he spent some time in Kurdistan to document the war. He talks to me about Abdul, about the lack of water, about the kids who play in the ruins and the tea they keep on drinking. He would have stayed longer if he could have.

These places I've never been to but that I've heard so much about, I have a hard time believing they exist. It's like they're loaded with meaning that isn't their own. The pyramids, the Taj Mahal, the Great Wall of China, I'd never be able to go without feeling strangely absent and removed. These places have too much history, and we've killed it by telling it, over and over. They no longer live. We fabricate this nostalgic past that has no basis in reality and we lie, over and over, selling these stories to poor innocent souls—but it's too late at night to be talking about stuff this complex. The photographer thinks so too. He isn't listening to me anyway.

I'd almost managed to forget that we'd reached that time of night, this inevitable moment. Do I have a boyfriend?

What should I say? I don't feel like anything anymore. He acts like he didn't hear, takes my head and moves it around in his hands. How do I get him to understand? Don't be fooled by my rosy cheeks, it's the drinks. Just the drinks.

They should rent out arms, bellies, shoulders, and necks to cuddle and hold the people who need it and don't have anyone to care for them. An affection business. The prostitution of tenderness would really take off.

Deep down, I'm fine with thinking my pain is unique and special, that I still have my own identity, that it hasn't all dissolved.

If you wanted a girl in heat, you should have picked someone else. I warned you.

I'm unhinged. There's nothing you can do about it, nothing you can say. I can pretend. I can forget myself, try to make him think I'm having fun. I must remember a little of what works. Bitterness pinches the sides of my tongue as though I've bitten into a rancid lemon. Stay, stranger. I can't handle another failure.

Do you usually like this? Please, don't rub it in. I should never have followed you. I end up telling him my life story. I can't help it. Poor guy.

It's always the same, every time. Every time they like me and I might like them too, I shove my issues down their throats like I'm the only one who's got any. There's no point, who wants to be stuck with someone else's baggage? I always end up at the same place.

And yet I keep hoping that someone might save me from myself.

I order an espresso. The coffee may be better three doors down, that place may even be more welcoming, but I keep coming back to the same café and sitting at the table in the corner, by the window. They give you little chocolates with your coffee. Just one, usually, but me, I get two.

I like the cups here. Little china cups with doilies. There's a smell of perfume, of powder, that makes me think of antique stores. Old photos covered in dust. Faces that no one recognizes anymore. A girl in a wedding dress who looks about fifteen. The waiter looks like a retired sailor in his little suit. I'll have to check if he has epaulettes the next time he comes by.

I pretend to read the newspaper. I try to get the gist of it. I only read the headlines. I get mixed up between all the politicians and their scandals. The president's wife who said something controversial. Siempre apoyamos a los agricultores. On the next page, his main opponent accuses him of saying the opposite. My predecessor left some English books behind in the apartment. I've been bringing them along with me for days when the paper is too heavy-going. I pull out *The Catcher in the Rye*.

I don't want to have to try to live up to someone else's expectations. Why does the photographer want to see me again? I have nothing to give.

He's decided he'll leave me in a better state than he found me in. I don't have the energy to try to discourage him.

He's only here for a little while. He likes sculpture, girls, guys too. He takes my hand and pulls me onto a bus without even knowing where we're going. We see the city and watch the people. He takes shots out the open window whenever the bus stops. He talks to me about lenses and exposure and how much he hates digital cameras.

I listen. It's the sound of his voice, mostly, that I like. He seems like someone who's found happiness. Or peace, at least. And it's that serenity that I hear through the stories he tells. I think it must make him feel good to believe that he's saving this crippled soul.

A bunch of seven- or eight-year-olds are running around all over the place. In the middle of the night, the city buses are full of kids playing, laughing. I feel like picking one up, sitting her on my lap, rocking her in my arms until she evaporates.

Sometimes, we sleep together. It isn't unpleasant, but it's empty.

Anke likes trains that arrive on time. She speaks in broken Spanish and plays in her submarino with a long spoon to make the chocolate bar melt faster, looking delighted. She hates the bus system, I love it.

I imagine that the two of us are in the same boat. Both of us, uprooted. Exit the stable, airtight social circle, where it's fine to judge a book by its cover. The two of us, reduced to having to beg for friends, to look for people who will put up with being followed around.

What if we're trampled in a riot because we didn't think to get out in time? What if we die here, what if we end up in tomorrow's papers? Hooligans. Anke hops up and down excitedly, talks about the star players, the coach who won gold at the Olympics once.

The sound of our feet reminds me of a military march. At every new level, more of our compatriots abandon us. But on we go, in solidarity, up and up toward the sky.

The players enter, tiny little pawns, and the crowd begins chanting back and forth. Cannons shoot giant confetti and red smoke. I wish I had a scarf. I could pretend I'm in England. It's cold and rainy in England. I'd need a thick wool scarf. Electricity in the air. Anke will be hoarse tomorrow.

The players run, sometimes. I have a hard time telling where the ball is. Did you see? Did you see that? She doesn't seem offended by my paltry performance.

Glasses overflowing with beer appear right over our shoulders. For the ladies, carried by hairy hands. For once, they're not trying to drag us into their beds; they're too busy. I have a fleeting thought about the photographer that quickly dissipates. The beer is sort of warm, the glasses sticky.

At halftime, I don't bother braving the crowd to look for the bathrooms. I spend the break squeezed between a kid eating a hot dog covered in mustard and his screaming mother. Still so much noise. The mustard stains the sides of his mouth, his shirt. When the game's back on, everyone stands up on their seats, a signal they all know. I have no choice but to get up too or I'll be left staring at the calves of the crowd in front of me. I can still smell the mustard.

There's confetti left in the sky and I'm reeling from all the people jumping up and down, stamping their feet on the rickety seats. I'm vibrating. I could almost fly away. They score a goal.

Far off in the distance, you can see the city skyline.

I scramble. I scramble so he'll think I'm happy. Kind of lifeless, no more no less. He doesn't know me any other way. I need to convince him. Not let him down, not make him feel sorry for me.

When he takes my hand, my heart beats harder. With anxiety.

Relax. Get comfortable. Breathe. He speaks to me softly as he takes out his camera. I'm petrified.

Now, focus on one spot in your room, on the left. Close your eyes. Take a deep breath. Now breathe out. Again. Forget I'm here. With each exhale, I push the pictures further out of my head. They come back again. I exhale harder. I know he's there. Thirty seconds, a minute, two. He's quiet.

I just can't forget he's there. I think of stone statues, statues that time and water end up cracking, breaking off in pieces and disintegrating. Statues, white and smooth. Plastic ideals of perfection. Statues, on boats, in museums, pillaged. Destroyed. On display for old Englishmen with stiff upper lips—the statues are Greek. The Greeks are dead. What happened to the muses? Now take a deep breath, and as you exhale, turn around. Look at me.

Click. Click. Click. Rest your cheek on your arm. Back up a little. Breathe. I have trouble swallowing. I do as he says. I feel more naked than I am.

I can't sleep. I listen to his breathing. When he took the last shot, I think I felt something. A pulse in my flesh. A fleeting moment of connection with the universe. Perhaps. My mind can tell me all it wants that my life'll come back to me, I still won't believe it. That quick flash? Maybe just a jolt, like when the hand of someone in a coma twitches when words of encouragement are whispered in their ear. He leaves tomorrow.

In theory, I'm here to sell tickets, or beer during intermissions, and to smile. Third shift, and I've barely sold anything. I start around 5, the shows start at 9.

The theatre's almost empty. It's way too early for the audience. It's time for classes in the rooms on the second floor. The instructors run past me with stacks of paper under their arms. A man shows up, crying. He comes up to the front desk. I'm all alone. I don't know him. He gives me a strange look. Sort of deranged. He seizes me by the hand, gets down on his knees, declares his undying love for me. He pulls me close. I resist, not knowing what to think. He's insistent. I pull my hand away. He explodes, his veins inflate, he pounds on the counter and the sound echoes throughout the lobby. How dare I reject him, after all that?

I'm shaking. He bursts out laughing, winks at me. Hey, new girl. I had you there, didn't I? He disappears, still laughing.

On that day in February, I let myself slide to the floor. The front door was wide open. It must have been minus 20 outside. My neighbour found me lying on the floor motionless. He wanted to call an ambulance. I said no, nothing the ER can fix. He set me up in the living room. Put a cushion under my head.

He came back later. He showed up with soup and tea. He didn't say much. Or anyway, I don't remember him saying much.

I've erased almost everything. From that week, that month, that life. I remember the neighbour. And the snowflakes falling all night long, glistening under the streetlights.

I counted them.

I guess I have trouble processing endings, good-byes, loss. My arms are full of holes. When I lose people, I stare at my empty hands and my cold bed and I realize that part of me is missing. That I've given them something I won't get back. No matter what I say. Even when I tell myself that I don't care.

I do keep a part of them, too. But it isn't enough. It's just this sad, pathetic consolation prize for losers. Because there's always someone else or somewhere else that matters more.

I wish they didn't go to so much trouble to win over these pieces of me if they're only going to leave in the end. Take one step toward me and I'll believe you. You don't have to say anything, I'll believe you. Forget the agains and the alway-ses. Whatever you do, don't tell me you love me. I'll get attached. You'll leave.

The photographer said you need to make the most of fleeting moments, to cherish them for what they were. But what he didn't say, what no one ever says enough, is that every dying moment kills a little. When there are too many, I get caught up in a crazy windstorm, hurled into the sand, the sky, the ocean waters. I end up damaged and drained and sometimes I don't want to get back up again. I just can't anymore.

The window in my room has shrunk. You can't even see the sky anymore through our birdcages.

No one seems to have noticed me come in. I push doors open, walk down a hallway. The building is so strange. I've been told so many horror stories about hospitals that I couldn't help myself. I go up, one floor is totally empty. There should be people. But there's nothing, it's abandoned. In one room, a bed, open closets, a Big Mac wrapper. I'll catch TB if I stay. Or leprosy.

On the third floor, finally, some noise. Doctors and nurses, busy as bees, buzzing around... I don't know who. Someone. I stand on the tips of my toes so I can see through the window. Some of the staff shift around, and I'm looking right at a man split down the middle, his jacket pulled up. His intestines spilling out over the side. Everyone's clothes are stained. A nurse wheels over a bag full of blood that she plugs in near the disemboweled man's head. The contents decant through a tube. The ECG looks dead. I'm hallucinating, my eyes aren't good enough to see all the way over there.

There's a smell, a potent mix of cleaning products and tissue fighting for its life. I can't hold it together anymore. My imagination's running wild. A stretcher rushes by, with a badly hurt child on it. The person pushing it gives me a look. What are you doing here, dumbass?

I should have gone with my gut and stayed home. It's not that I don't like Anke's friends. That's not it, I don't know them. I don't want to know them. I don't even feel like drinking. The cat here is in the same boat. But he's spitting on them. If you don't have anything, we can lend you something. This ridiculous pink wig and these leopard-print leggings.

Cat, talk to me. Do you eat paper birds? You're not answering me. I could go for some candy. Little rum balls from that bakery that's closed on Sundays, to be precise. You know the one? You're purring.

How many times have you died? Have you been to cat heaven? What's it like? Are you a guy or a gal? Not that it matters, I meant no offense. I can tell your ego's fragile.

You know how toast always falls butter side down, and cats always land on their feet? If I tie a piece of toast to your back, butter side up, and I throw you, what do you think'll happen?

You're gonna bite me, right, that's what'll happen. You a house music fan?

Doesn't look like it. What are your thoughts on the Iran deal?

For a moment, I dreamed that the dog ran away. Better yet, ran away and got hit by a truck.

In the middle of the night, I happen upon a tired, quiet vendor who stands out from the shouting neighbours and the smell of fried food. Spread out in front of him are garlic, newspapers, porn DVDs, and toothpaste. I stop, hoping to see someone buy all those things at once. I'd follow them home, just because. I'd take down their address.

The vendor sighs without looking at me. He seems gentle. Shy, almost. Does he like those overly sweet croissants? He reminds me of the summer I almost sold hot dogs. The guy who would have hired me carried himself in the same kind of way. I wonder how my life would have turned out if I'd ended up selling hot dogs that summer.

On Sundays, vendors of all sorts set up shop in the street and a huge crowd of people swoops in to invade. To buy, but also to people-watch. Come on Chloé, you have to come. There are street artists, dancers, clowns. It's full of junk, antiques, and clothes. From stuff you'd find in your grandmother's trunk to amazing designers who'll be big in Milan next year. You have to tip-toe around to avoid knocking over the books, or the huge piles of toy giraffes blocking the path. Not easy to find the perfect outfit in the chaos, but I have a seasoned pro with me.

Here, look, this would look good on you. Try it on. Yes, perfect. Take it. This too. The designer is so cool. He makes clothes with these huge wooden buttons on them. That one, though, too big, hangs all crooked. What's most important is that your clothes fit you properly. You know what I mean? I've won a day of shopping with a per-sonalized stylist. Two of them, actually. Adriana and Matías seem to think I'm behind the times.

They throw a bunch of clothes at me that I don't even have time to look at. They're on a mission of utmost importance: get Chloé dressed before she pulls out her Power Rangers shirt that smells like mothballs. Or worse, something from last season.

Adriana met a guy yesterday. Another one. He spent the night thinking she was great. She won't call him. He won't call her either. He flirted just enough to make her give in. She held him off long enough for him to take up the challenge. She tells me this as she rips the polish off of her nails. To play into this dance of bodies, you have to make this mutual pact—pretend it's true, that it's serious, but still accept that it'll be over tomorrow.

Simple things always end up complicated. They're scary. She must believe in the balance of the universe and convince herself that some-where along the way, happiness leads to shitti-ness. So she pretends that the present is good enough for her.

Matías isn't talking. He looks like he's looking out for something, or someone, right in front of him. He hasn't touched his juice. Without warn-ing, he jumps behind us and crouches down to hide. He pokes his head out every fifteen seconds to check if he's been seen. He looks ridiculous. I don't know what he's hiding from, but he'd be less obvious if he were jumping around waving a big red flag.

I like to think he's hiding from a ruthless mercenary. Matías's men, the few that I've seen, are straight out of a fashion magazine. When I see one, I have to repress the urge to reach out and touch him, scratch him, to see if the wax will pill on him, like those apples you buy out of season that are a little too red.

I never have time to get to know them enough to check, to scratch their arm and see what comes off, I don't do it. The other morning, he locked one out. Poor guy came to see me to ask me to come down with him. I didn't think to tell him that someday, he would find love.

The one standing in front of us is handsome, but not like a red waxed heart. He's kind of scary, even though he must weigh 135 pounds soaking wet holding a brick. He scares Matías too, apparently. His nails suddenly dig into my shoulders. Matías whispers to us, that's my ex, we're still in love, but one of these days we're gonna kill each other. Last time, at a party, he said he wanted to get back together, and we couldn't keep our hands off each other and, at the end of the night, I went home with someone else without explaining myself. I never called him back, even after he left me 13 voicemails.

I burst out laughing. I can't help it.

Matías and his blond angel. A cow being led to the slaughter, resigned, by a sadistic child wearing shorts and a striped shirt. A shiver crawls up my back as I watch them leave. I can still feel Matías's nails digging into my neck and shoulders, his joints locked. I don't know anything about their past, but I imagine it goes on and on, endlessly vindictive, with low blows, possessive love, jealousy, and tears, and a few good times sprinkled in. Because there has to be a reason it keeps going. They stay stuck on it, without really knowing why, and maybe they're right.

Matías turns to us, pleading. We give him the nicest look we can, to encourage him. I won't ever see the blond angel again.

I ran marathons every day down the long, dead-end hallways of my adolescence. When a boy got close and tried to love me, I pushed him away, trying to get out while I could. Love was the worst of all words. The word that didn't forgive. The word that needed to be avoided at all costs if you wanted to stay alive. He must have been crazy, the boy who hadn't learned that yet.

The boss keeps pacing back and forth between the theatre and the street. He doesn't look at me as he passes by my counter. I try to capture his shitty attitude on paper. Make yourself useful instead of screwing around, come help us! I didn't know helping build the set for the new play was part of my job description.

We have to take the seats out and replace them with these big cubes. They're yellow and red, dirty, we'll have to clean them too. The chairs fold up, take that end, we push them to a door, a new play, all set, bits of wood, cans of paint. ¿Venís? Apparently he's physically incapable of not mumbling. I feel like taking his fat face in my hands and tickling him, but I'm not sure he'd appreciate that.

Emilio won't stop fidgeting. It's his play that's being put on, the first he's ever written and directed from start to finish. He's worried about how the audience will react. He wants every single line to be understood, for them to feel the depth behind even the most trivial parts. Did he do a good job?

I don't know if it's because he feels bad about the set-up debacle, but the boss comes by my counter right before the play starts. Everything in order at the front desk? I saved you a seat if you want, on the left just as you come in.

It's the first time I see something that someone I know has created, in a real theatre. And not just any theatre. I sit on one of the cubes that I busted my ass to set up and try to catch the audience members' eyes as if to boast to them, you know, I know the director. Milking the fame he doesn't even have yet. On the verge of giving up, a drink in hand, while a complete stranger gloats about their New York friend's extraordinary exhibit, I'll talk about how Emilio put on an experimental play at the Galpón that's managed to redefine the essence of art. A magical evening, I have no words to describe it. A shame you couldn't be there. His approach is fascinating. A triumph the likes of which we haven't seen in years. I wouldn't be surprised if this were to launch a brilliant international career.

I'll emphasize the 'a' in 'fascinating' every bit as much as they stress the 'x' in 'extraordinary.'

The scenes play out one by one, rhythmically. A woman runs from one end of the stage to another. The play takes place on all sides at once, sometimes right in the middle of the audience. Maybe the story is supposed to take place in the future? The people sitting on some of the cubes stand up, they're actors. Others take their place. A guy I recognize from somewhere takes notes, holds his pen in the air when he isn't writing. I don't see Emilio, he's probably backstage biting his nails. Funny idea, having people practically sit on the floor like that, on seats without backs.

A gong rings out, and six actors stand up, facing us in silence. They take off their clothes and throw them into the room. Their skin green under the white light. They stare at the audience for a few long, awkward minutes. Enough to create a palpable uneasiness that they stretch out even longer. A couple of soft coughs in the audience. An actor finally emerges from backstage, dressed as a robot. Another bang of the gong, and the six start acting again, naked, like nothing happened.

Emilio, the cast, the boss, their friends, they're all here. The robot too. He's cute underneath all that makeup. Very cute, actually. Even with the little bit of eyeliner left under one of his eyes. He asks my name, sits close to me, whispers sweet nothings into my ear. Ezequiel. I blush, I don't know what else to do. Pitchers arrive, that awful server from the tea garden too.

¡Caaariño fue fantástico, estupendo! ¡Qué genio que sos! And she plants an obnoxious kiss on Emilio's lips, leaving red marks behind. Speechless for a moment, he finally says gracias, Gloria. Gloria, right, that's her name. She looks at me. Glares at me, more like. Finally she places me, I get a half-smile.

Gloria. She takes me back to that lily-scented garden. Cold, arrogant, feline. The only woman from this country that I've exchanged a few words with. Ezequiel fills my glass and taps me on the shoulder, ¿querida, te quedaste colgada? Yes, lost in thought. The air is heavy and dark. We raise our glasses. I like bars where everyone's squished together.

How cold is it where you come from? I'm startled. Ezequiel's hand slides onto my knee, even though he's pretending to be passionately engaged in the conversation next to us. I wasn't expecting Gloria to talk to me. Ezequiel has the name of a prophet.

A name that makes the room shake, that'll end up in history books. Gloria is waiting for an answer, maybe she's genuinely curious about my polar country? Where I come from, it's so cold your nostrils stick together and, um, your eyelashes too. I point at my lashes. I confuse them with the word for eyebrows. She corrects me, another smile. I can't tell if it's forced or not. I think I'm gonna visit, one of these days. But I'm scared of the cold, and the bears. Are there a lot of bears? She mimics a bear.

Ezequiel suggestively whispers in my ear that Canadian bears don't scare him, lets his hand slide up along my lower back and then goes over to join a group of friends who've come to congratulate him.

Emilio is beaming. The premiere is out of the way, he survived. I try to see if there's anything left of his fingernails. There's a constant swirl around him. Gloria throws a couple of looks his way. He's busy holding hands with a girl I've never seen before. He pulls her onto his lap and says something in her ear. The bare shoulder of the girl right in front of his eyes. Her face gets closer and closer to Emilio's. Is he only seeing Gloria?

To my right, a discussion gets heated. Alone among a bunch of strange faces, with the familiar ones all busy or gone, I have to be charming, brilliant, dazzling.

They single me out. I'm rich. Oh really. Life is so easy, isn't it, far away from home. Throughout their conversation, my new friends keep saying, you know, for people like us in the third world. Ah, the third world. On the other side of the equator, the champagne flows like a river and people are so happy, sure. I can *choose* which country I want to live in. They talk about their poverty with an arrogance, a pride that's hard to take seriously. There are poor people here. Too many of them.

They're not young, beautiful, well-dressed. They can't live off their art. The drinks loosen my tongue and I snarkily tell them I wish all my new friends a suburban bungalow, a minivan, two blond kids high on Ritalin, and a pool in the backyard. A cliché. That's all they deserve.

Waking up, startled, to the leftovers of insomnia, moist sheets, almost falling off the bed, the vacuum again, this feeling that it wasn't all a dream, that I stabbed someone to death, is this really my room? ¡Ay lo siento! Querida no sabía que estabas. Pero Chloé, levantate, ya son las once.

Carmen takes me aside at the end of dance class, you missed the last few weeks. Why? A boy? I don't even have a chance to answer her before she starts ranting furiously. Never sacrifice your life, your practice, your art, for a man. You'll wake up one day, fat, ugly, tired, having given him everything that mattered, with him gone. Your in-laws will pretend you never existed when you show up at a dinner to confront him— they'll call the police, they'll call you all sorts of names. You'll have nothing left. You hear me? You'll just be stuck wiping the asses of a couple of kids, you'll have nothing, nothing but broken dreams and a giant landfill where your heart used to be. Nothing accomplished, you'll be empty. Too late to start over. And you'll see what you wasted your life for. For nothing. Nothing. So think carefully. And don't miss any more classes! I look at her, dumbfounded, and I note to myself that I've made pretty impressive progress with my Spanish.

She puts on her usual face and goes back to leading her life with an iron fist as usual. At the back of the room, behind everyone else, I ask myself whether it's possible to let everything go, for everything to slide off our backs without piercing our skin.

And I wonder how much you have to go through before it becomes impossible to recover.

After the cookies, Adriana's decided she's getting into sewing. Little dolls are pinned to all the purses here. With a few friends, she'll have a booth at the artisan fair outside a music festival. She has to make an army. She'll barely sleep. I hope she hangs them by their necks in her display. You want one? Not sure why, but I say yes.

Different fabrics cut up into half-doll shapes, scattered near the sewing machine that she picked up at a bazaar recently. I admire her patience. After stuffing them with cotton she puts on the finishing touches. In the end I stay and help her sew on the eyes. I only give them gouged-out eyes.

I've seen *The Birds* twice. The first time, I fell asleep, I was 13, a boy was rubbing my back in a big bed. The second, I was alone, maybe 17. I've been scared of crows ever since.

In a recurring dream, I'm in a big space that's been invaded by them. I can't move. I can't even formulate the idea of moving. There are more and more crows. My legs won't do what my brain is telling them. The crows get closer. They surround me, start fighting amongst themselves.

One of them goes for it, I watch it come at me like it's in slow motion. I know it's going for my eyes, that it's going to devour me and leave nothing but my bones behind. I know the rest of them will follow. I can't do anything. I can't cover my eyes. I'm a statue, an offering. They caw. I hallucinate eyeballs being ripped apart by their beaks. Then they roll onto the pavement, covered in blood.

Cold sweat, short breath, startled awake, disoriented.

You still hanging in there, Betty? You don't move as much as you used to. I hear you whistle sometimes when I'm pretending to sleep. I didn't know you could whistle. Have you seen my notebook? Do you think you may have taken off with it sometime without noticing? They say it's going to rain tomorrow. Be careful, don't stay too close to the window. In case it really does.

The beast is staring at me, rolling around on its back. The garbage can has been knocked over, its contents spread all the way out to the living room, leftover spaghetti and orange peels pouring out of its mouth. The walls are stained with old sauce. Damning evidence that this is the work of a hardened terrorist. Jesus Christ, you stupid dog.

I grab the dog and try to put a collar around its neck. It licks my face, tries to climb up all over me. You stink, stop drooling. It takes me four tries. The roommates laugh at the improvised circus, bet on the dog three to one. I struggle all the harder. This fucking animal. I'll get it out of here if it's the last thing I do.

At the park, a man with a dog comes up to me. It's never ladies who come up to me. Some people like ugly dogs. His is nice-looking. I think I'll trade with him. I don't know why he would agree to it. They say we have the dogs we deserve. If we trade dogs, do we trade merit?

I let the beast off its leash so it can play with the others who are running free. I do nothing to hold it back as it races toward a colossus three times its size like a kamikaze pilot, barking a war cry. They fight, and mine ends up being ejected into the air. It lands at the foot of a tree, its face against the trunk, dizzy and bloody. Tries to get up, stumbles. Stupid dog.

Officially, The Prophet Ezequiel came over to see Emilio. He makes the walls of my apartment shake as he materializes. I'm crazy about his name. Everyone hide. Be afraid! The long-haired red-caped superhero is here to punish you, to shine the light of truth on this depraved city. Leave this body, Satan. Order will reign over this place before Judgment Day. Bad guys will be punished and the meek will be rewarded. With a technicolour background that follows him around like a halo. You can't be named Ezequiel and be mediocre. I mean, you can. But it would just sound wrong.

I have a nobody name. Ezequiel is a prophet. Chloé isn't a name with a complicated history full of obscure references that we'll never really get to the bottom of. I have a name that goes unnoticed, not one that evokes miracles.

But Ezequiel. Ezequiel has no idea he's a hero. He loves our dog. He pets it. I tell him to take it home with him. Even though it isn't mine, I'm giving it to you. Then come back and tell me how much you still love it. I'd be so happy not to have to share a home with a monster.

He doesn't care about my dog park story. He approaches me, puts his hand on my thigh, picks up where we left off. I dizzy him with words to give things time to fall into place. He makes a path under my shirt, I keep going on about whatever. He finds it funny when I say ¡Maldito perro! ¡Que anda a la concha de su madre! Stays in character. I play my own. I've stuck a mask to my face, a mask of a little girl who's been bested by a pathetic dog. He wears the mask of a boy who thinks he's a man. He must think I need a strong man, and that he's that strong man. He says, come over to my place if you don't want to sleep with that dog. I promise, there are no monsters in my apartment.

We start kissing and Emilio shows up, looking annoyed. Come on, we're late, it's time for rehearsal.

Ezequiel ups and leaves me. Without giving me his number, without taking mine.

I spent a long time watching snow fall, that week in February. I could find nothing better to do than stare into the void. What's the point of thinking?

The snowflakes in the window looked like fluff.

You're just a stain, Betty. No one has ever wanted you, you've never been desired. No one cares about you either, there's no one who depends on you. No one remembers what you do, or what you like. No one asks you why you're in this country. Your existence has no bearing on the world, not even the slightest impact. You're useless, unnoticeable. How does that make you feel?

I turn my back for one second and the streets change direction. I've been walking in a straight line for half an hour and this is the third time I've passed this place. Everything looks seedy. More lived-in debris. Zombies.

Even the call girls on the flyers you see pasted on phone booths here are zombies. The classic Pampitas, Daysis, Brendas, showing off their tits and asses, they all have bloodshot eyes and hollow cheeks. All around me, zombies—some screaming from the windows, others inside roasting chicken.

I could add the zombie-escorts to the collection of girls on the fridge. It would be lovely. A nice addition to the game the roommates are playing—find the same pictures but with different names and numbers, pile them up, biggest pile wins.

The garbage lid won't close anymore, the flies are having a party, Luz hasn't come. I don't know where the bags are. I don't know how to ask. I don't know when to take it out. I don't know where to bring it. I really wanted to do it, this time. Stir-fried vegetables. I just burned the rice. All charred and stuck together. A smell of burnt popcorn in the apartment. Couldn't find coconut milk. Or spices. Or tofu. There's no one here. No one.

Never anyone when I need them. I'd let them know. That tonight, I was cooking dinner. I sit on the lid of the trash can. It bounces back up. As soon as I lift my butt off, it opens again, springing, happy. I start drumming on it with clenched fists, like toddlers throwing a fit when you take their toys away. And I let myself fall over, next to some leftover ribs.

We're all blindfolded. We need our limbs to be touching. Resist, sometimes, or let yourself be guided. That's the only instruction Carmen's given, I don't know what I'm supposed to do. Thankfully, no one can see me. The pressure on my back builds. I feel my bones rolling on hers. Slide, turn. I search for a spot that I can lean on. Ezequiel, if only you could be pressed up against my bones like this. Find yourself an excuse to make my apartment walls shake.

Everyone stop, stop moving.

Standing on one foot, my leg bent, the other in the air, her hips against mine. Focus only on the point where your bodies are touching. My muscles seize up, a long line of tension crosses my back diagonally, I start getting these spasms in my right leg. I'm not breathing anymore. Everyone stay focused, listen to each other.

I bet you've never seen a sleeping giraffe.

Emilio and I left the party at the same time. I don't like you going home alone, he says. Outside the city zoo, he gives me a look that says I'm not game. No lights, no cops around. Just watch me, I grab the fence in front of him, he has no choice but to follow. He knows the zoo like the back of his hand, he's spent hours in front of the reptiles and hippos. I don't know my way around in the dark.

The path barely leaves the trees. We zip along, hiding from imaginary security guards. The owls are watching us. I can hear them.

Emilio gets me back for my bravado by running too fast ahead of me. Tree leaves smack me in the face. I wouldn't be able to find the exit without him. I think we're near the tigers. No time to look, I end up grabbing his hand, so I don't lose him.

Everything's different at night. The animals come out of their cages and inanimate objects come to life. The line between what's acceptable and unacceptable bends a little. Everything we take for granted can fall apart. He jerks me to the right. When he stops, I fall on him. This is where the giraffes are. We can't see anything. But we stay to look anyway.

It's really bothering Emilio. He hesitates. He scrunches up the tip of his nose, moves his shoulders around. Querida, is that really what you want? Emilio frowns as he gives me Ezequiel's number.

The torero is a strong man who can do it all. He waves his flags to dazzle while the blood flows behind him. He puts on a great show. A handsome man, proud. He wears out his adversary, sends him flying into the stands and blinds him with fury before finishing him off.

In the arena, the blood of the vanquished spills, just like the sweat of the victor. It's the smell that excites them, however many there are. The corrida is one of the oldest forms of mass entertainment. Its exact origins are hard to trace; they've melted into humankind. Contrary to popular belief, it's still practiced all over the place.

But not here. Here, there are no bulls in the corrida.

I call. A metallic voice answers in Spanish that the number I've reached is not available.

I call again. Same thing. Three tries, three strikes. I don't understand how phoning, or dating, works in this country. How do I know if the codes are the same? I still don't know if there's a common denominator that unites us. I can't distinguish the culture from the individual. Is it him? Is it me? Is it this place? I don't know how to play at love anymore. I mean, I guess I never really have.

Flies really are social creatures. They hang out in groups, gather to fly around together, land together. Like girls going to the bathroom at parties.

I pick one, and the hunt is on. I follow it, armed with a rolled-up newspaper and all the determination I can muster. They're fond of windows and green plants, this one dives in under a leaf. The fucker won't make it out alive. But it's hiding, the little rascal.

I climb up onto a chair, onto the table, I follow it with my gaze through the apartment and I run after it, shouting war cries. This one won't get away. I'll fight it to the death. I try again with the next one. I leave little carcasses on the ground, but the apartment's still swarming with insects, the strongest ones, the biggest pains in the ass.

The word for waiting in Spanish is esperar, the same as hoping. As in, you can wait for something to happen, you can hope it will happen. But it's far from guaranteed.

My time is too slow. It crawls along in never-ending minutes that don't pass, that taunt me. I want to explain to The Prophet Ezequiel that there's nothing less constant than time.

He needs to know that time is elastic. That two days have gone by without him even noticing in his busy, full existence, but that to me they stagnated, endless. But how can I tell him that if he can't be bothered to pick up? I keep trying. What do I have left to lose?

The pitcher has deformed the silly girl since she slid into the arms of that boy.

His name is Marcelo. I wish he were wearing a tank top. Un marcel. I wish the girl were wearing a bright yellow dress with a white lace hem. Or for someone dressed up like a giant bunny to come wish me Happy Easter and bring me a bouquet of roses made of chocolate, skipping through a field of dandelions. Today isn't Easter. Matías is high as a kite. He's screaming into my ear. I can hear you! Stop yelling.

The scene is set. Still life. I like that better than the French, nature morte. Dead nature, that scares me. It makes me think of cemeteries and dried-up flowers. A life that's still, that's much better. Closer to something real, something that lives. ¿Me comprás chocolate? I ask Matías, trying not to get my hopes up. He starts licking my earlobe.

Emilio didn't come home last night, neither did Adriana. The other morning, new sandals appeared in the entrance, not really Adriana's style. And a purse beside the shoes. Gloria? Emilio's door stayed shut for a while.

I could learn to knit, to pass the time. I can see myself with a pair of needles in my hand. I could make a little coat for the dog. Or little pompoms for its ears. Ezequiel would come over to see. I'd make a sparkly pink outfit. I'd embroider "dog" on it. Unmistakable. I'd find a little bell for its neck, so it can call Ezequiel over. And then, if there's any wool left over, I could strangle the stupid mutt with it.

Every time she goes to the flea market, Anke finds treasures like toasters, teacups, paintings, and furniture that would make an antique dealer die of envy. All I see is a pile of old junk.

She pulls me over to a booth where a vendor is standing with his belly sticking out, looking like an Elvis impersonator. A bunch of faded vintage posters around him. One of them, in German, tries to attract the tourists of its day to their own version of the Alps. Instead, Anke shows me an old wall phone, with the receiver still attached, hidden under a pile of boring shit. Western Electric, Made in USA. It must be from the 1930s! Fifteen pesos. How did it wind up here? What are you even going to do with that? But the vendor looks at Anke like the phone holds a secret he'll take to the grave. Or, like he knows how to make a sale.

They silently come to an agreement. He carefully wraps it in newspaper, taking the time to read each page first. I start getting antsy. When he's done, he asks ¿de dónde son? Without even waiting for an answer, he strikes the same pose, the one that makes him look so funny and yet, at the same time, so profound.

The flies. Again. It's 4:07 p.m. I lie down, close my eyes, roll over in bed, think of fresh vegetables, tangle my feet up in the sheets, then think of something that I immediately forget, roll over onto the other side, free my feet, roll over again, pull the sheets back up, sit down. It's still 4:07. I call my superhero again. He doesn't pick up.

Hey dog, did you know that forty million years ago your ancestors looked like weasels? What does a weasel look like? They're ugly. I also learned from this encyclopedia that small dogs live longer than bigger ones, but that it's the ones with wrinkled, scrunched-up faces that die the quickest. You look like you rammed face first into a wall the minute you came out of the womb.

You see, it's not all bad news.

Betty. Beeettty. Betttyyyyyyyyy. It's hot, I have nothing to do, nowhere to go, tell me a story, yes, the same one as always, it doesn't matter, what else do we do but tell the same stories anyway. You're pouting. Fucking princess.

The evening sun paints the room with golden light. From Anke's window, you can see a park, children, balls. Everything is slow. Her roommates come home. Milly, Kike, hi! Kiss kiss. They'll be back later, they have errands to run. Anke puts on Cat Power and switches the kettle on. She flips through a novel, I try to read their news. I still never understand any of it. The words, yes. But the rest. The majestic teapot is placed at the centre of the coffee table, with two different cups, the cookies carefully placed on a decorative plate. I could take a picture, but I don't know what I'd do with it. Outside, the kids keep chasing after the balls.

The evening is mild. The pasta's good. The airy bread that Kike brought home is passed around the table, I finish my glass and it's refilled immediately. Milly wears earrings that make her look like Audrey Hepburn. How was the trip home? The plants in the planters are dead, which doesn't seem like Anke. I missed the mountains. The mountain air, you know. Anke seems like she should have a jungle on her roof. It's the most beautiful country in the world. This city must kill plants. Anyone want beer? But you left, you don't live there anymore. Give it here, I'll open it. The bartender from the other night tried to impress Milly with flair moves. A few girls crowded around him and he missed his shot. Milly laughs, if only I could have said something utterly clever in Spanish!

In the hammock, a relative silence envelops me. The city lights, prisoners of the smog, keep the night from fully setting in. Like flashlights behind a frosted dome that covers us, coddles us.

All of us, trapped in the dome of madness. Little bits of conversation go on around me. Have you ever felt like you're always half somewhere else? I read somewhere that the constellations are different in the southern hemisphere. Sometimes, I tell myself that two people looking at the same star at the same time are linked together. A cosmic connection, or something like that. Even if they're far from each other and don't know it. It's silly, I know. I feel that way too when I dip my toes in the ocean. Other feet, on the other side of the world, in the same water.

Come, says Kike. He brought a Bukowski book. I was doing fine on my own, staring into the void. He reads some of it out loud. I like Bukowski, as long as he isn't talking about horses. Kike doesn't speak English. I can't follow his mangled accent. But the mood this evening makes me want this to last.

We're just missing a few candles. Sitting on a roof in a city that stretches out to eternity makes up for it.

When he puts the book down, I grab it and read on in silence. Too shy to recite it, the words get stuck in my throat. The world disappears as I dive between the lines.

So, what are you going to read to us? Me? Nothing. Here, you're better at this than me.

Matías comes back from Brazil with three bottles of cachaça and a sunburn. He takes out all the glasses in the apartment and pours huge shots into each of them. Themed evening, he walks around in a floral bathing suit. Blasts the music. The apartment gradually fills with tanned dudes. Where did these guys come from? Cloiiiiiita, Adriaaaaana, come here, my loves, I've missed you!

He shows us all the new dance moves he's learned. He tries a few steps of the lundu—that's what he says it is. Adriana pretends she's the Carnaval queen. Someone rips three leaves off the tropical plant in the living room and puts them on her head, sticks them in her ponytail. She doesn't mind. She and Matías take turns stealing the show. The others won't be outdone. A little train starts shaking to a beat that goes like boom-a-tch-a-ay-boom-boom-tch. It's definitely not Brazilian. Hands travelling across everyone's asses. Chloé, you're bored! Drink this. And this. Show us your samba moves!

I'm tipsy? More guests keep showing up at this impromptu party. The mood is hot hot hot. ¡Caliente! They've turned the living room into a dance floor. Someone pulls out a broom and decides to start a limbo contest. I didn't know that was still legal. Yep! Yep! Yippie! Ay ay ay. Liiiiiiiimbo time. Some of these guys are gonna have headaches tomorrow.

They line up. The bar starts off high. The first one approaches and bends over, leaning forward. Shows his ass off, tries to sway the judges who are holding the broom. A few whistles. Different hemisphere, different limbo rules? He isn't disqualified. A girl goes next. She goes at it more traditionally, but as soon as she's under the bar she starts shaking her tits like she's in a music video. Someone pours her a caipirinha from overhead, she opens her mouth but most of it falls onto her chest. The next guy doesn't even go under the broom. He goes around it and tries to give the judges a kind of lap dance.

I'm having a blast watching them.

A hand appears, puts my drink down on the table and pulls me onto the dance floor. Matías. The music changes, I'm in a *Flashdance* remake. He acts like a ladies' man, doesn't even give me a second to think about it, spins me around. It's way over the top. I play along. The couples around us do the same. People exchange partners. Skin against skin, hips against hips. Change partners again. The whirlwind goes on, effortless. Never a misstep; they've been dancing all their lives.

I fall into Emilio's arms. I don't know where he came from. A little awkward. Dancing isn't really his thing. He plays the game but I don't buy it. Holds me back a little as I pull away, laughing.

Good party last night? I told them, the chicos, to be gentle with you. I'm gonna give them a talking-to.

Luz can try all she wants, they're not here. Unless Matías is still sleeping. Which one did he pull into his bed? Which ones?

She's gotten her hair dyed. It's not that it bothers me, but it makes me curious. There are red highlights that weren't there last time I saw her. Luz, looking cute at the hair salon. It makes her look younger. More elegant, more alive.

I have a hard time imagining her there, gossiping with all the ladies with curlers in her hair.

Wanna grab a drink? I had forgotten about The Prophet. Does Matías have something to do with this? Emilio?

Of course he wants to see me again. He's sorry, he never got my messages. Who told him? He goes around the front desk, slides an arm around my shoulders, kisses me. I let him. I was chasing him, after all. In my memories, he was more gentle. More handsome.

One of the actors will be hospitalized for an illness of some kind. Ezequiel's been asked to replace him. A European tour, a shot at the big leagues. Isn't that amazing? It's with one of the hottest directors out there, his dream. I can't seem to muster any excitement for him. What did he do to see me again?

He talks to me and I see him now, full of shit, pretending to be someone else. He's just a phony, taking his place on stage now that the first guy stepped down. His performance is so over the top, so fake. He hasn't even bothered to camouflage his schtick. The spectators leave one by one, they've had enough. They paid for a moment of truth. He doesn't understand. He just stands there like a puppet, an actor unmasked. I had dreamed of something different than this.

Better off just focusing on his pretty eyes. That's what I'm here for, anyway. My hero Ezequiel, don't tell me it's not true. Don't tell me you're no prophet, no knight in shining armour. That you have no supernatural abilities. You have the name, but where's the rest?

At the bar, Ezequiel places his hand on mine, kisses me and bites my bottom lip. I'm scared my mind might be playing tricks on me. I don't want to find myself limp at his side, viscous and shapeless, and have to suffer the shame of a body that stops responding to its head. He isn't responsible. He isn't dangerous.

How's Emilio doing? Why is he talking to me about him? What did you think of his play? Seriously, you can tell me. Even Emilio didn't dare ask. It was good. I didn't understand much. Spanish, you know... He smiles. No, it was really great, that's not what I meant. I like your accent, it turns me on.

I could kick his teeth in.

He ruined everything, my prophet. I free up my hand. Don't go anywhere, I'm going to get some beer. I should leave, admit defeat, admit that I'm hollow and useless. Go let my heart bleed out somewhere else.

He comes back, a glass in each hand, a glint in his eyes that takes me back to that first night, when he talked to me about Canadian bears. He leans in toward me. The drinks. The drinks, again.

I throw myself at him. All around us, people are happily chatting amongst themselves.

They've probably all just come from the theatre next door. Sometimes, from my balcony, you can see Orion's belt. He places his finger on my cheek as he tells me this. In the middle of the city? One of his eyes is blue, the other more greenish brown. A tiny mole just above his upper lip. He downs his beer, tastes good. So?

Now that the initial shock has passed, I surprise myself by laughing as though I still know how. My laugh cascades in the night we've left behind us—I can't seem to stop him to say wait, listen. It's been so long.

He lifts me off the ground, keeps kissing me. Ends up slamming me up against a wall. I hear the stitches of my shirt rip. I feel his bones grind up against mine and I squeeze him harder. He licks my neck, my ears. I bite him. He slips his hand up my skirt. I'm wet. Finally.

Come on, I live nearby.

I land on the pavement like I'm landing on a broken dream. He doesn't understand at all. My feet, heavy. My head too. Too bad, Don Juan. Even forgetting has its limits.

He forgets all about Orion, gets me a glass of water, confident that this is a done deal. Could we maybe do some shots? In the reflection in the window, I see him take his shirt off.

I really want to want to be here. I need to want to be here. I want to be here. Come on, grab onto that bit of laughter before it slips away. Up close.

He touches me. I shut down.

Are you okay? What can I answer? What I should say is hit me. Hit me, you'll see. I won't feel a thing. Come on, hit me. It'll be funny. What, are you scared? I'm gonna laugh. I said hit me. Till I bleed. You want to know if I'm still alive? Really let me have it. You'll find it funny, I know it.

I don't say any of that. I don't say anything.

I'm not sure how much instability it's appropriate to dump on people.

It's shameful, not wanting someone. It's an insult to Eros and the other modern gods; desire is the first commandment. I'm unable to obey.

Waiting, with an open mouth, to be dissolved. Flogging myself till I bleed. Hit me. Really hit me. What would he have thought? I spent the night at his place anyway.

I doodle people being hanged and beheaded, and little kamikaze bunnies in action on my paper placemat. Dynamite fastened around their waists. A torn ear. Un conejo asesino. He'll take us all down with him. There isn't enough room to make everything blow up properly. Anke doesn't laugh. Why not? It's funny, no?

The bombs, the bunny, ka-boom?

I ended up making a little crack in my bedroom wall. Betty feels abandoned. I try to reassure her. Make no mistake, Betty, a crack and a stain aren't too much of a support network. Anyway, it's barely a crack. More like a fissure. Just don't think about it.

I burn my fingers on the steaming cup of tea. Luz took pity on my pale complexion. Drink up, it'll do you good.

I look at her, and I look at her life. What I understand of it from the early aging of her hands.

Woe is me. The rate of depression in amoebas has to be pretty low, right?

I count the flies that circle the stove, and my cup. I try to kill them without moving anything but my arm. Fate really has it in for me. It's vindictive. It's probably a good idea to light some candles as a reminder that I'm thinking of it. That I fear it. Shrines aren't for nothing. There's a fine line between fear and respect. Fate inflates itself with fear, thinking it's love. It's no better than the rest of us.

I partially renounce my immobility and throw together a makeshift fly swatter. I strike at random. They're everywhere. I line up their corpses on the table. I try to make a straight line. Perfectly straight. I take out a twenty and roll it up tight. Then, I blow.

It's my birthday. I don't tell anyone.

Some people are just really good at being happy. And I should be happy for them. You've got a knack for happiness. Congratulations, well done, lucky you. How do you do it? That's some accomplishment. Gotta cheer them on, tell them to keep at it. But it's so much more tempting, from where I'm standing, to throw it back in their faces.

Afterward, sometimes, I'll regret it. I shouldn't have done it, I shouldn't have thrown out those words to tear him down. He'll be left with burned hands, stinging eyes, he won't know how to protect himself. But it'll be too late, the damage done. There's no use apologizing.

Tonight, I don't feel like going out with Anke on a tour of appetizers. I spend all my time going to vernissages and meeting guys who bore me. She said 10 p.m. at the centro cultural. I show up late, people are happy and perfect, carefully distributed around the space as deliberately as the objects in the paintings. But something's missing.

I don't feel like pretending.

I don't even try to look at all the pieces. I get more and more tense. Fixated on this idea that nothing is okay. And that it needs to be said. I go up to different groups of people without talking to them. They don't react until I finally shout at one of them, ¡falta algo!

What what what? they all quack back. What do you want? Nothing. Everything. To push the limits. To live. I can't accept that life is nothing more than the sum of these long, dragged-out days. Even worse, because all of you, you other people, seem fine with it. They smile at me politely, like they're saying my rage will pass, eventually. Like them, I'll calm down and understand the virtues of a quiet mind. It's inevitable. You'll see. In a few years, you'll be the first to run for comfort. We were the same at your age. Stop looking at me like this is a teenage phase. Stop reassuring yourselves that you made the right choices, stop telling yourselves there was no other option but the mold. You just don't want to go down with the sinking ship alone. You're wise, and you're dead. All of you, dead.

One of them finally says, you want to kiss a girl? Is that what you want?

I make my way over to the plaza with the obelisk, the city's central meeting point. People endlessly repeat the same waltz. Meet up, kiss, leave. A nice, happy ritual.

Two old ladies holding each other in a long embrace. Sisters who haven't seen each other in forever. An exile. A cancer remission. This other guy came to buy coke. He paces around his scooter, looking agitated, until another dude, looking just as nervous, comes by. They part ways right away. Two other people are getting their pictures taken in front of the obelisk. One of those stupid photos no one will look at. A girl sits down to knit. She barely finishes four rows before a man comes to join her with a banjo. He puts a foot on the bench and starts singing. The ritual comes to a halt for a moment so that people can listen.

The boy who's been sitting across from me for a while finally comes up to me. Can I walk with you? That's nice of you, but not tonight. He offers me a lollipop and then disappears. It tastes like cough syrup and stains my tongue, like sweet red lipstick.

I watch the waltzers. I come undone, little by little, as I watch them spin around and around.

I surprise myself by dancing alone in my room. Without music. I can't really move without hitting something, but that's okay.

Sometimes, I need to keep my hands busy with inanimate objects. I write a letter with a thousand beginnings and no end. Never an end, never a middle. I can never get past the first few lines. I sit there, staring at the damn page, without finding any answers or questions, getting swept up in a tornado of images I thought were long forgotten. What is it that keeps me stuck here, stuck nowhere?

The popcorn is disappointing. Too wet on top, it doesn't even look like butter. They should say oil, would you like some oil on your popcorn? Stop lying. Why do I keep buying it? I can't stay focused on the movie. The couple in front of me are making out really loud. You know there are houses for that? Hotels. Cars, even. I'm not in a state to put up with other people's love. Morality, modesty, manners, we came up with these things because happy people piss everyone off.

Do you really need to let everyone on the planet know that you've found someone to swap spit with?

Behind the dressing rooms, almost hidden, is what looks like a garden. I have the day off, but I still end up at the theatre. The tomatoes rotting on the vine keep me company. They say that crying cleanses. Water filling up, then emptying. Backwash, basically.

The door opens, I don't react. I'm sleeping, my head between my arms. It can only be the boss. Why can't I find a place to myself? He sits down beside me, I'm scared the table will fall over. Everything can't go wrong on the same day, right? Would you rather I leave you alone? At least if he's at my side, we won't have to look at each other. Why didn't I realize that this was already his hideout before I discovered it? He looks as lost as I am. Do two wounded souls make a whole? Like two wrongs making a right?

That's what I'm wondering. If so, what happens to the other soul? What does it become? Does it just dissolve? Does it gather up the combined woes of the two? Pick which one of you will pay for your happiness. Does tragedy just pass itself back and forth? Nothing created, everything lost.

The boss doesn't say anything, neither do I. The soul is one of those absurd things that get heavier and heavier as they break.

Hey, what's your name? You must have one. You can't just be "the boss" all the time.

Pablo. My name is Pablo. He lights a cigarette and I don't tell him the smell makes me nauseous.

Matías pushes the door open. With bags under his bloodshot eyes, his clothes all crumpled. It must be a week now since he was home last. A bruise on his arm, a fat lip, and I don't want to know what else. I hesitate. Adriana told me this has happened before. He looks thin.

Finally, I walk up to him, and he still doesn't react. ¿Matías? I take him into my arms, but he doesn't even seem to notice I'm there. We fall slowly to the ground. I'm not brave enough to ask any questions. His blond angel, I imagine.

It's over. I don't know if I'm happy for him. I kiss his hair and softly hum in his ear.

The main purpose of lullabies is to numb. To make you forget.

I can't decide. On the shelf, the pasta and polenta are one on top of the other. Many different brands of each. Different colours. But mostly red, blue, and yellow. Almost never purple or pink. I never see those colours at the grocery store. Hands reach out and grab boxes and bags. Pasta more often than polenta. You have to bend down to reach the polenta.

I start compiling statistics. Red seems to be a popular colour. Women are more likely to pick the polenta than men. They're less afraid of bending over? They take a lot of pasta too, though. Now that I think about it, there are just more women than men who go grocery shopping.

I recognize the guy in front of me. He keeps a low profile at the theatre. I don't think he teaches classes. Maybe he works the lights? We've been introduced, but I forget his name. I'm bad with names.

I say hi as I walk by him. Chloé! What a surprise. I'm only used to seeing you behind the counter. You're not buying anything? No, I always come to the grocery store so I can leave empty-handed. He ends up inviting me over for dinner. Points to the box in his hand, ¡será polenta!

187

What strikes me most about him is that he has a certain stiffness in his back and, when he walks, I feel like I'm watching a ghost go by.

He makes me think of a teacher at a country schoolhouse. I wouldn't be surprised if he lived with his mom. That stiffness in his back, maybe. He offers me candy. I think they're dragées.

I've never really known what dragées were, but looking at the platter he hands me, I tell myself that must be what they are. He holds them under my nose, insistent, and I don't even think to make a joke. No one understands my jokes anyway. His apartment is dusty, everything's old. He pulls up a chair for me and just leaves me there in the living room. An aria starts playing, preventing any possibility of conversation.

I realize it's too late, now, to ask his name. Especially since he compulsively repeats mine every time he speaks. ¿Caramelos, Chloé? ¿Te gusta el país, Chloé? Over the lull of the opera music that's playing, I wonder what I'm really doing here, apart from just killing time.

On his bookshelf, a bunch of obscure books I've never heard of. I pull out one about demons in the Middle Ages. Upsetting pictures of women hanging by their feet. The book cracks every time I turn the pages. I'm not even sure this is in Spanish. Is this Old Spanish? The calligraphy is incomprehensible.

If I were you, I'd put that book down.

His tone is ice-cold. On the table, slices of fried polenta on plates. With nothing else.

Dog, have you ever wondered if lemmings give suicide any thought before they throw themselves over the edge? There are some questions modern man can't answer. Great scientists, somewhere out there, are weighing up lemming questions. Some would even have us believe that lemmings don't kill themselves. That there are voracious eagles or some other hibernating predator, like zombies, that periodically decimate lemmings. They come crawling out of the woodwork, hungry for lemmings, then go back to their world once the population has been regulated for another few hundred years. Smoke and mirrors to evade the essential question: do lemmings die intentionally or don't they? The other question being whether the intentionality changes anything at the end of the day.

Have you ever thought about that, shit for brains? There you go wagging your tail. You think I'm taking care of you?

I know what you're missing! One of those cones you get from the vet to keep you from scratching your ears. You'd be perfect with a cone for sick dogs. You'd get it caught on all the furniture when you run, you'd spin around, not knowing where you were. We could sneak up behind you and shake the cone to make you shut up. A cone-dog, clown-dog, dumb-dog, wow.

Adriana introduces me to Pedro and his cousin, Fede. Pedro is a sailor, he's going around the world on his boat. No, not Pedro. That one's Fede. Or is it Pedro? Bueno, da igual. She's wearing a scarf on her head, tied under her chin. Sunglasses and lips like a starlet from the '20s. Neon nails.

I halfheartedly say oh really, cool. And Fede is a lion hunter. I sit down. Of course. Kittens, I mean. Fede is a lion hunter who hunts kittens. Grrrr. León, gatito. I don't get it.

I motion to the waiter to let him know I'm not ordering anything. Adriana's hand slides quickly up and down Pedro's arm. He winks at me. The sailor's not bad. So, Pedro, do you have a tattoo? Excuse me? You're a sailor. Do you have a tattoo? Adriana starts laughing. Fede jumps into a long explanation of the history of taxidermy.

Betty, when's the last time you saw the neighbour with that tragically rebellious lock of hair? I hope they haven't moved. I'd only have pigeons left to look at.

Nothing wrong with pigeons, but it's just not the same.

Emilio looks up from the couch he's fallen asleep on. Adriana, wearing heels that anyone else would have a hard time keeping their balance on, with nails to match her eyeshadow, a colour that complements her lipstick and dress. She's so shiny you'd expect a trail of glitter behind her.

I have two invites to the Bonbon Cherry show. Can you imagine! Lucky me. Emilio pouts, dubious. Me too. We look at each other. I surprise myself by smiling too candidly. A moment of complicity I wasn't expecting. She has a look on her face that says You two deserve each other. Both so lame, why do I even bother anymore?

I feel like it's been weeks since I've seen Emilio. He's all wrapped up with Gloria. Reduced to voices behind the door. He waves me over.

Move over a little so I can sit. He turns to me and props his legs up on my lap, then lies back down. I can't move anymore, I'm stuck in a trap. What are you up to these days? Asking that or asking anything. He leans his head back, looks up at the ceiling, shrugs, sighs. ¿Y vos?

I was little, the Oka crisis had shaken the world. I would watch these blurred images, a bridge, tension that bordered on hysteria. On top of the machine guns on the news, they'd bombard us with stories about the poor reservation kids getting high off glue and gas and permanent markers. They were about my age. In the garage, I waited until everyone was gone and opened up a tube of wood glue. If it was good enough for them, it was good enough for me.

Such a disappointment. The world had made false promises, of dreams that could never be.

On the church steps, tourists fly by without stopping. I'm drawing, but they move too quickly. A girl sits down, finally. She reminds me of Gloria. The leggings, maybe.

The girl looks at her phone nonstop. It doesn't seem to be making her happy. She wiggles back and forth from one butt cheek to another. Rummages through her purse. I try to capture her on paper. She puts the phone away, takes out a mirror. Is she waiting on a call from a lover who's stood her up? She plunges her hand back into her bag and rips out her phone. Dives back onto it. I have a hard time making out her facial expressions from here. I imagine she's angry. Trapped in a treacherous universe. Where even phones break their promises.

I don't want to stay too long in front of Matías's door. Or look at it. Or knock. What if he picked that exact moment to come out? I don't detect any movement behind it.

I put down the chocolate heart I just bought him at the grocery store. I don't know if he'll understand it's supposed to be a joke. Or if he'll come out before it rots. Cuidate amigo, I write next to it.

Plant, we need to give you a name. You too, crack in the wall. Look at that, my room's a full house now.

Señorita, you're so pale.

A stranger's hand lights the cigarette that's between my teeth. I lean over a little to reach the flame. The man's hand strokes my cheek. And the smoke escapes, smooth. I'm wearing gloves and a tight, low-cut dress. My infinite eyelashes brush against the man's hand when I blink. The street is empty. Apart from the man, who wears a tailored suit. His hair greased to one side, a hat. We're close to a metro entrance. Hot air climbs up my thighs. For once, my nails aren't black with pollution. Nothing sticks to my skin.

I would savour the smell of the match being struck. That would erase, for this short moment, the smell of the cigarette. And I'd take the stranger's hand and never look back.

I go to the theatre, pretend to be busy. I bring a book and set myself up at the front desk. I feel a bit less guilty than I would staying at home doing nothing.

Emilio walks by, surprised. What are you doing here? Do you feel like coming upstairs?

They're 8, 9, 10 years old. Sitting nice and still in a circle. They seem to be making up stories with their hands, they barely look up when I arrive. Everyone, this is Chloé. She comes from a country full of polar bears and today she's going to join our class. Obviously, the bears feed their imaginations. There's one kid who sits off to the side. Kind of chubby, clumsy. He wishes he were somewhere else, he's always the last to figure out the exercise. Emilio leans over and whispers something in his ear. The kid stares at me, eyes straining hard to believe the unbelievable, laughs, looks at me again. And he joins the group again with an energy I hadn't seen in him before. He stops every fifteen seconds to stare at me. I imagine that in his eyes I've become a rhino tamer.

Wait up. Emilio looks through the costumes, an old bolero, a stuffed python, African masks. We're gonna play. You might even like this. Yeah, I don't think so. The sacred circle. You can scream or make noise, but no words. Didn't I have something to do downstairs? He gets in my way and stops me from leaving. Emilio! Leave me alone. Some other time, okay? He takes my hand. Then the other. He starts waving his hands. I resist. If there's one thing I don't know how to do in life. We're two warriors. Preparing for a ritual. He pulls my arms up in the air like a bird preparing to take flight. My eyes pointed up toward the sky. Are you done? He keeps it up, more and more determined. And, consequently, so do I. I try to pull my hands away, but not hard enough. Every time we land, the iron staircase resonates with a clang. Stop! Someone's going to come. I don't want people to see me like this, Emilio, stop. I try to sidestep, he cuts me off. Shakes his head No with the big paper maché mask on. I giggle.

Then I burst out laughing. A stifled, nervous laugh. He keeps jumping. I told you you'd like it. Jesus, Emilio. If Pablo comes up, I'll die. If someone finds out, if you tell anyone. He starts moving back and forth from right to left, pulls me along with him. A rhythm. He's ridiculous. I'm so pissed. Emilio, I swear, I'm leaving. And yet, when he lets my hands go, I don't leave. He's panting. Pounds his chest and screams. High pitched, then low, then a growl, a croak. He jumps up and down with both feet, takes my hands again and pulls me with him. I'm gonna kill you for this! It would be my pleasure, he says back.

It isn't surprising in this city to see artists moving from place to place stained with paint or with a blowtorch in hand. Still, stumbling upon a big plot full of huge sculptures made out of scrap metal, right in the middle of a residential street, is unsettling. Lunar Park. A mix of dinosaurs and robots, if you have to call it something.

At first, when I saw the letters, I didn't understand. They're arranged all crooked, the R in Lunar has basically fallen off. Makes the whole thing even quirkier. Normally, I zip by. I prefer that to looking like the girl who's never seen a commune, or that came to do some casas recuperadas tourism.

A frail-looking girl with green dreads and ripped jeans calls me over, says come, they won't bite, before disappearing inside. I stay where I am. As far as I'm concerned, the sculptures make great guard dogs. People come and go. Some weirder than others. Most pay no attention to me. On top of the giant robots, a mop of wool hair gently sways in the wind. Their heads follow. When the street falls quiet, I hear the wind blow between the sheets of metal. Some mysterious force compels me to sit and listen to the improvised concerto. A little kid comes to play in the tall grass between the statues. I realize that whole families are probably squatting here too.

The wind keeps whistling. I convince myself that they can't see me. I don't know why. I don't know why I get up, either. Or why I head toward the door.

I hold my breath. I'm scared animal entrails will drop onto my head. I wonder if people back in the day set up a ritual to calm the Stonehenge gods. I keep going forward, carefully, as if that may help for some reason. There's just a fake soldier I have to confront, at the entrance. A robot like the others, with an army helmet and a captain's badge pinned where his heart would be. His face is like the Joker's. He threatens the innocent passersby with an inquisitive finger. Nunca más, is what's written next to him. I slide behind a skinny guy who's on his way out, the door gently shuts behind me.

On the fourth floor, a painter. I'm normally indifferent to abstracts, but his really grab me. Something about the density of the lines. I sit. The studio's empty. Apart from the painting in front of him and the space it occupies. He's completely focused. On the concrete floor, two tubes of paint, a few brushes. His back is turned, there are no windows. His painting slowly takes shape. A strange feeling of peace, of abundance, emanates from him. Nothing like the supercharged energy of the squat. Here, nothing exists. I'm not even sure he knows I'm there. I await his next movement, suspended. Black and white on the canvas, unsettling density. I forget that I'm not part of it. I forget that I'll never be part of it. And I travel with his brushstrokes.

The line that runs from his hands to his back is so pure it almost excuses the rest.

On his way out of the studio, he says there's more than one way to inhabit silence. He slips across the floor and disappears. The huge painting, maybe finished, watches me from the wall where it takes pride of place.

I wouldn't know what to say about it. Nothing like "magic, soothing, whole." Nothing critical or intellectual. I spend hours sitting on the floor of the squat, losing myself in it while no one bothers me.

I want a flower crown. I want to roam the city streets like I'm a little girl. I wouldn't notice the disapproving looks of grandmas or the fat, wet air kisses of the workers. I'd keep my head high and be proud. I wouldn't bring a doll with me. I wouldn't have a bleeding forehead from the thorns, and no one would applaud as I walked by.

I've been waking up later and later. The dog is barking. An alarm, somewhere far away, goes off. I hope the thieves make off with the car quickly. I hope it stops. I hope the noise stops. All this noise. Always, noise, too much noise.

Noise that sets in and never ends. An endless drone. Everywhere, day and night. In this crazy city where nothing is ever silent.

Betty, have you ever believed that rain was the sky crying? Not me.

Llover, llorar. Pretty similar, though.

Come on, please, do it for me. I don't know any-one who speaks French. Come on, Chloé! Under different circumstances, I might enjoy Emilio begging me like this.

He wants a girl to speak French for the soundtrack of his next play. There's no script. He suggests I write a few words. Nothing too com-plicated. No one will understand anyway. You must have something that you wrote at some point that you can use? A poem, or a song?

How do I explain?

What do you want me to talk about? Improvise. The tape recorder stares me down, there's no way I can forget it's there. Betty, what would you talk about? I've never written a poem. I definitely won't be starting today, that's for sure.

So this morning I got up, it was late, I was sick, Luz was still there, I don't think she noticed, Emilio showed up full of pep, threw the tape recorder at me like it was something fun, said alright, see you later.

Of all the dangers in Colombia, it's falling asleep under a palm tree that terrifies him most. Falling coconuts kill more people than the guerrilleros. Anke's boyfriend tells me this with the straightest possible face. What, you've never thought about coconuts falling? It's the epitaph I'm imagining.

I feel like going there to get killed by a palm tree just so my tombstone could read Here Lies Chloé Duclos, who died from too much dreaming. Palm trees go hand in hand with the ocean. With children slathered in sunscreen, with pink lemonade and cars with sun visors that say Florida Beach.

Palm trees aren't weapons of mass destruction. No matter what wimpy boys think of the coconut rebels. And Anke throws me under the bus, takes his side, but yes, Chloé, the palmeras kill people. She's gotta be kidding me. You'd know that if you'd done a bit of research on South America. It's not because she's sleeping with a Colombian that she's palm tree expert all of a sudden. She's never told me about him. How long has this been going on? People who are afraid of everything usually die getting hit by cars crossing the street on a green light. Did you know that? Did you also know that holding hands for too long significantly increases the risk of pancreatic cancer?

Finding boys cute. Finding just one boy cute would be enough for me. I'd love to get butter-flies in my stomach whenever I see him. To tell myself, here, him, maybe. No need to talk, smile, nothing. Sharing an invisible instant, making the moment last, leaving it suspended in time. Even if it's just for a little while.

I feel a pinch in my stomach and my head turns without me even realizing it. I look at this one, him, as opposed to someone else. He stops, his silhouette becomes clearer. I understand, but can't explain, which detail struck me most.

The boy who holds me here, wide awake, screwed tight into all the layers of the present.

Pigeons are fighting over the breadcrumbs that an old lady's throwing at them. They circle the bench she's sitting on. They charge without mercy. Their little bulging black eyes, their feathers swollen beneath their shivering skin.

In all the chaos of pecking, some are aiming for their brothers instead of the bread. Their fat, smothered cries sound like human wails.

Whatever happened to bird songs? Another lie.

An inexplicable cold spell: four days, an eternity. The thermometer flirts with the freezing point. Humidity gets into your joints, gets through the windows, through clothing. The whole city is sick and erratic. It's all people are talking about, even Pablo.

The Public Health Minister gave the flu epidemic a name, the W. Stay home, don't go out, don't go to work, don't go around kissing anyone. The calls for calm on TV are followed by hysterical stories with titles like "A Biblical Plague" or "Cryogenic Attack." Everyone running around like chickens with their heads cut off.

Some walking around with surgical masks on, some barricading their businesses, others boarding up their homes.

The problem isn't the cold, it's the world's escape through little cracks it shouldn't fit through. Forcing them to admit that ultimately, they're not in control. And it's total chaos, everyone hide!

After 4 p.m., I allow myself to eat ice cream straight from the tub, even if it's not mine. I make random rules like that, impulsively, when I feel like justifying my urges. I declare new ones that contradict the old ones. I wish I weren't ashamed of all these goofy laws I pass.

What I like here is that I can order ice cream over the phone. It shows up five minutes later by scooter. If I want, they can even make me half-half tubs. It's the same price for two flavours.

As usual, Gloria doesn't even look at me when she comes into the theatre. I greet her enthusiastically. ¡Hola! She pretends not to recognize me. I double down. Coucou! Hellooo! She turns away and sticks her nose into a magazine. Gloria! This is getting ridiculous. She has no choice but to say hi. Do you want me to go tell him you're here? If I go on any more she'll spit on me, beautiful Gloria. I pretend to dive back into my book. I watch her out of the corner of my eye. It's true, there is something about her.

With the little chubby kid from the class clinging onto his legs, Emilio comes downstairs, without acknowledging the additional weight. Bueno, Paco, nos vemos la semana que viene. The kid won't let go. He's such an odd one. He still needs a push to get him through the door. I wonder what Emilio thinks of all this. He looks happy to see me, happy to see her. I can't tell how he sees the two of us.

Gloria's attitude leaves little room for interpretation. But he doesn't hurry, and keeps her waiting. The sound of the squeaky stairs resonates in this silence that weighs heavily on at least two of us. He comes back, it doesn't even seem like he went to get anything. He wishes me a good evening as he leaves. I mutter an inaudible

suerte through my smile. In her closet, next to
her 36 pairs of leggings, she's got a skin-tight
Sailor Moon outfit, heeled combat boots, a club,
and false eyelashes. A sophisticated futurist tig-
ress. Stay off my turf. Got it?

What are you doing Saturday? The boss has never shown interest in my life outside the theatre before. Have you ever been outside the city? Emilio and I were saying we've got to take you to the Delta. And the Galpón will survive without you? I'll come get you at nine. Nine on the dot, don't forget.

The doorbell wakes me from a dream. Saturday, already? Pablo! He really is excited about this cottage of his. My mind in a daze, I almost fall to my death down the stairs. As it watches me tumble, the dog disappears under the armoire, but can't fit all the way underneath. Its ugly mug looking even more beat up than usual. Stupid dog. Stupid fucking dog. Emilio runs all over the place with his shirt half-on. No more ready than I am, he grabs a banana. Want something to eat? Gloria's here.

She savours the element of surprise. I can tell by the look she gives me. I'm too asleep to react appropriately. Pablo is ringing the bell like a madman. The dog barks. From the open window, we hear him yelling. Okay! Calm down.

We all cram into the double-parked car. Emilio abandons me, so I'm stuck with her in the backseat. He's too kind, really. The engine running. If Pablo turns it off, I'm not sure it'll start again.

About time you showed up! Gonna wait till the tank was empty before you came down?

There's no way out. In front of us, the road's blocked by a bunch of protesters. Behind us, total gridlock, more cars stuck in the same trap. We haven't even made it eight blocks, we're off to a great start. Pablo hits the gas every once in a while, in neutral. He coughs a little to try to hide it. But apart from that, nothing. I actually imagined he'd be more impatient. He doesn't even start drawing up plans to have the car teleported, or make the slightest sadistic joke. Gloria uses the stop to adjust the rearview mirror and fix her hair, an elbow on each seat.

She leaves me behind, naturally.

If it isn't the farmers, it's the workers, the ice cream shop owners. Against the mines, against the government, or because Pedro didn't feel like going in to work today. Every day there's a protest. Here, all problems get solved by people shouting in the streets.

Listen to us. ¡Escúchanos! You can't pretend we don't exist. A hundred times, a thousand times, a million times the same face affirming their faith in democracy. They march past us, their white knuckles clenched around signs that echo the things they're tired of yelling.

Meanwhile, up above, the rest of them sip their scotch and play cards. This law, do you think it'll pass? We should keep them busy with something. A flu epidemic, there you go. Call Marina at TV7. Create a commotion around a strain that's mutated, another inexplicable, dangerous outbreak. Really play up the hysteria. Tell her to focus her story on a kid who died from it. They don't even have to try to be original.

Go get another bottle, Giuseppe's coming over. If they keep it up, we'll make a statement. We'll say the situation's under control, that we're working hard on it and yes, as promised, we'll enforce that federal prison law. Hurry up, Giuseppe gets cranky when there's nothing to drink. And when he gets upset, I don't have to tell you what happens.

Pablo, Gloria says to tease him, I didn't know you had such a shitty car. Had I known, I would have stayed home.

If you want, there's still time to drop you off. I don't know, maybe you could go on a shopping spree. You must have friends you can see. Why did Emilio bring you?

He could have at least given me a heads-up. So, I've heard you know Ezequiel? I didn't see that one coming. Gloria thinks she's already won. We've known each other for years. We tell each other everything. The whole car is quiet, everyone listens attentively. The men want to know. What does she know? I'm not sure I'm any good at this girl stuff. I told him, you know, that he should give you a chance. You seem really great. He can't always be with supermodels. You probably just don't know how to play it. I tried to convince him that a normal, nice, simple girl would do him good.

My cheeks catch fire. The bitch. What am I supposed to say? All eyes on me. Ezequiel... They're waiting for the rest. Funny thing, what happened between us.

Or what didn't happen, I should say. When I told myself I wanted to see him again, I went to ask Emilio for his number. He didn't want to give it to me. I had to insist.

You remember, Emilio?

It was really embarrassing. Can you picture it? Me, begging him to give me his friend's number, and he keeps saying no.

Did you give me the wrong one on purpose?

I whisper to her, can you believe it? All the same, these chicos. They want a harem of girls fawning all over them. They want to feel like we all worship them. The more of us, the better.

Ridiculous, right? How are we supposed to feel special that way? And I say it again, louder, every time I'd call Ezequiel, I'd get someone else's voicemail, and I didn't even realize. I thought he really didn't want to talk to me. But I had the wrong number all along. When he finally got in touch, the whole phone tag thing had been so complicated that I'd lost interest.

I think I'd prefer it if wars between women played out the way other wars do. We could fight it out, slap each other, and pull on each other's ears. Instead of this endless scheming, these invisible battles, layer upon layer of dirty tricks. Whispers behind each other's backs, echoed and escalated, spit into faces. But no blood, so no pain, right?

Outside, cows and fields and a few trees. Yellow hay.

I've always loved watching the autumn leaves fall. There's something about October skies. I have this reflex where as soon as I have a leaf in my hand, I rip all its skin off. Until there's just a skeleton left, stripped clean, a nervous system gently collapsing in on itself.

The sun's yellow reflection on the hay is gonna end up burning my retinas.

It's the first time I've seen Emilio worked up like this. You okay with the knives being over here? Or would you rather place them yourself? Is this good enough for madame? Do you want me to fold the napkins up into little triangles, too? I didn't do anything to calm the situation. I subtly encouraged him to mock her, went as far as touching him without making it look like it was on purpose, kept going until she lost her shit. If they were playing water polo, they'd be scratching at each other underwater, nails sharp as knives. Red blood in the turquoise water. I'd swim in it.

Your sauce is inedible, you trying to make us choke? Would it have killed you to listen to me? For once. You had to put twice as much in just to make me look stupid. Great job. If they're trying to play an old married couple, their performance is flawless.

I bask in the soothing sun. My feet hanging over the end of the dock, just like in the Beau Dommage song. The song starts playing in my head. It's been so long since I've heard a tune from Quebec. They all left me on my way to this place. I tap along to the beat of this song that no one can hear but me. I can't even hear the birds sing. Nothing but this song fills my head.

As soon as I dip my toes in, they disappear. My toenail goes in and little particles cover it. The whole front of my foot, erased by the brown water. I smell algae, it doesn't matter. I don't know if it's brown from pollution or sediment. Maybe that doesn't matter either. The little ripples that take off from my feet slowly die out, sink all the way to the bottom.

The gates of Hell are supposed to be underwater. The gates of Hell, what a joke. Caught up in these stupid details.

Pablo makes the wood crack with his giant feet and construction boots. The dock isn't wide enough for us both so he sits on the side. Throws a rock into the water.

His waves conquer mine. A little shake-up for a few seconds, waves crashing against each other. The brown water regains its composure, becomes smooth again, heavy.

Ever since Anke fell in love, it's like she no longer exists. She met him and melted into him. They'll stay that way, glued together, until they explode. Like all the others. They float along, convinced that they're whole now, that they're above the rest of us. Is this Hollywood's fault? Fairy tales? I'm stuck in a world that won't stop pushing this idea that one is bad, and two is better. Two, the only goal. Two, the golden number. Who's ever said anything else?

I know Anke showed up on time. I know she's patiently waiting for me. That she brought a book, and hasn't ordered yet. A serious book about something important. A book you can proudly show off in the metro to tell everyone else look, this is what I'm reading. Under their breath, some might add that it's way better than those dumb bestsellers of yours, the rest of you, who probably don't know the difference between Orson Welles and H.G. Wells. But Anke is classy. I haven't even left yet, and she's already there.

I have nothing to wear. Everything's dirty. Ugly. I can't decide. Go out, or call her. She's waiting for me. I pace in circles without even pretending to get ready.

I'm sick of the *Goldberg*s. Enough already!

He asks to use the washroom. It's too late for classes, too early for a show. The theatre's closed. The man insists. I want him to leave. End of the hall, on your left. He comes back. There's no paper. What does he want me to do about it?

Can you call the janitor? I don't know where the paper is kept, or where the janitor is. Has the entire universe turned against me? Please leave. His expression changes. Self-importance takes over his greasy face. Excuse me, miss, do you know who you're talking to? What, are you a member of the all-powerful incontinence club? Pablo shows up, out of breath. Señor Gutierrez, I didn't know you were coming today. He stands between us and adopts a fawning tone that doesn't suit him. Pablo, I don't wish to pry into the theatre's internal affairs, but you may want to review your hiring process. The man speaks with all this floury language even in casual conversation. Pablo starts waving his hands around, blushes. Apologizes for me. I can tell he's furious that I've made him lose face like this. I'm a stupid gringa again, a little insignificant thing, hanging around, not understanding a thing. I don't run to go get toilet paper, I don't lick señor's posterior, and I don't apologize. It's Pablo who ends up going, practically dragging himself across the floor. She's new. Go fuck yourselves.

I should have known, maybe, that it's risky to offend old white men who strut around so confidently in fancy suits.

In the living room, Emilio, with Gloria. I quickly grab some cookies and a bit of cheese.

From behind my closed door, I can still hear them too clearly. They're making plans for the evening. Their discussion gets buried by kisses and dog whines. Then their sounds quiet and come to me in whispers, punctuated by bursts of laughter.

In the hole, my paper airplanes have been reduced to a sort of pulp. With remnants of red flowers adorning their tomb. Melted together, no wings or noses. Maybe a tree will end up growing out of them.

A tree, Betty. With big white birds flying all around it. Do you think there's ever been such a thing? They could carry me out to the fake outdoors. I'd go, you know. Caught in the talons of giant birds. It wouldn't even bother me that it isn't real.

I rip out a sheet of paper and make another airplane. And again, it falls without even making an effort to fly.

Is it actually possible to slip on a banana peel? That's the kind of thing people say without really believing it. Who's actually seen someone slip on a banana peel? I demand proof. Just saying it's a thing doesn't make it one.

I throw one onto the floor and jump on it. Medium slippage, smashed peel. I try again, making less of an impact. Slight skid, peel destroyed. A third time. With a lot of effort, I manage to fall. It doesn't even hurt. No bananas left to sacrifice. Don't really feel like going to buy more. The dog digs into the puree, excited. Gets it all over itself, spreads it all over the kitchen. I'm so disappointed. The risks actually posed by banana peels are hopelessly overblown. At least now I know. I have to look elsewhere.

Betty, I'm so fucking sick of this. How can you be satisfied with so little? Why? Can you please tell me why?

I dressed up slutty on purpose. Short black dress, fitted but not tight, the neckline just loose enough for the straps to slide off my shoulders a bit, pointed heels, red lipstick, black eyeliner. I sit at the bar, alone. I look at them but don't smile. I down four shots of tequila. By the fifth, a hand places itself on top of mine. Let me at least buy you the next one. He's not cute. I imagine he's from Russia or Moldova. Moldova, that's exotic. I don't even know if that's a real place. I decide his name is Evans. He places two glasses of whisky in front of me. And the same in front of him. The second one is for good luck.

He likes sailing. He'd make his sailing outfit burst at the seams with those big arms. All the little stitches, snap snap snap snap. Is he hairy? "Sailing," maybe that's a sex position he's talking about. I'm sure he makes children cry when he tries to smile and he squishes spiders with his fingers. More shots. Vodka this time. I don't know what he's talking about, but I'm laughing.

Getting up feels like a bomb got dropped on my balance. With both my hands, I grab his arm, which he might have been holding out for me to take anyway. The dance floor. He pulls me close. Are we dancing? A song plays, then another. I'm losing myself, my head in his chest, my eyes closed. Little spots, like fireflies, wandering around. Softly, gently. As far as I'm concerned, I've always been here and I'll never go anywhere else.

On the floor, shapes start to blur. I bounce around, let myself be carried by the tide. He holds me up, pulls me, I barely realize the songs are changing. My back brushing against strangers' stomachs, my chest against their backs. I join the crowd, dive into the sweat and drool. Evans, with his brutish arms, elbowing people. I think this is the moment I've been waiting for all my life. If I jump, maybe they'll catch me and have me crowd surf, take me to the end of the rainbow. I'd pick up Lucky Charms with my fingers and sprinkle them over them, over us. Dissolved into fine snow, golden dust. Inside, outside, everywhere.

If only I could jump high enough to get past their outstretched arms and lie down in their hands. With the air sparkling and Evans carrying me, with the crowd carrying me.

Men, mostly. And smoke. A sauna of cigarettes. Evans buys me a drink. The alcohol tastes like water with just a subtle aftertaste. Martini, maybe. Where's he dragging me to? He knows his way around. The bar counter is sticky. The white shirt of the man next to me, transparent where it's stuck to his wet back. The same ugly face as Evans. He buys me another drink. I only smell cigarettes. They probably have rats here.

I have to go to the bathroom.

I knock into a few chairs. And the men sitting on them. Grunts. There are so many chairs. I can't find it, I go all the way to the back, along the walls. I knock over a few chairs, they fall without a sound. If they do make a sound, I don't hear it. Where are the washrooms? I have to—I trip, almost fall flat onto a table. A man, furious. ¿Los baños? I yell. I mumble. He pushes me in the opposite direction, points to an even darker corner.

I can't see a thing. Too dark, too drunk. Where's Evans? ¡Evans! ¿Evans? That's not his name. Dumbass, he won't know that's him. I don't know where I am anymore. Forget the washrooms, I have to get out of here. Now.

Gripping onto the forest of chairs like a vice.

Tighter and tighter. I can't move without hitting a chair. They've added more, they're everywhere. I start knocking over the empty chairs, throwing them onto the floor. They're conspiring. Still no noise. Too many chairs.

They push me. Dumb bitch, go do that somewhere else. Stumbling around on my too-high heels, holding the wall. Nauseous. I get it all over the place. I get back up, my head a little clearer. Our feet always lead us home. No matter what state we're in. I repeat that to myself like a mantra. Close to home. Almost there. How many metres since I left that cave?

I gather what will I have left and drive straight ahead. Good thing I have this wall. A garbage can falls. Is that me? A cat? Is someone following me? Too late to try to understand how and why objects keep appearing. Where did Evans go? I hold myself up with both hands, puke again. My nice shoes must be full of it, they aren't mine, what will Adriana say?

I'm sure my hands are pissing blood—no time to worry about that. I run. Trip. Who's behind me? The wall is so hard. So crooked. Come on, girl. Hurry up. More noise. Voices. Evans? I manage to hit the garbage next to me. Hit? Pet it, almost. I have to run faster. I have to find somewhere to hide. The police? Definitely don't turn around. Shit. More steps, voices. How many lanes are there? How many cars? I cross without looking. Without knowing where I'm running to. Not the slightest cry comes out of my throat. Am I standing or lying down? I was running. I'm running. The pavement is soft. There must be cars. I have to get out of here. I try to move. What's happening? A voice now, just one, I can't move a muscle. It's this city. People, suddenly. Everywhere. But no faces. They approach me. I still can't cry out. They touch me. Everything is white and fuzzy. I should be able to scream. Lying starfished in the middle of the street. Stuck there, cemented into the pavement. Someone's breath. Red. What's happening? Run! Try to catch hold of something, I don't feel my fingers anymore, or my legs.

On all fours on the cold bathroom tiles, my head hanging over the toilet bowl, a hand rubbing my back. I puke again. Water. I want water. Jesus I'm weak. Emilio comes back with a glass. I splash it onto my face, neck, shoulders, hair.

He takes me, rocks me slowly, sitting with me on the ground. It hurts, but I don't have the strength to tell him. Or the strength to be anything but a ragdoll. With one finger, he wipes away a silent tear. The last thing I remember is falling in the street. Was it a street? After that, nothing. Emilio stays with me, calm. He whispers in my ear, shhh, está bien.

I wake up in his arms, in the same place, the same position. Like time hasn't moved at all. A little wet round spot on his shirt. He runs me a bath and leaves me. In the mirror, I look scary. I think of everything that could have happened to me. Was I drugged? I drank so much.

Betty, look at how I've ended up. Look at how fucked up I am. You knew it, you say. Do you remember the princesses?

The ones I dressed up 300 times a day. A new dress every time. No touching, they had to stay nice. Sitting there, all happy. All in a row next to each other. Their smiles trapped in their plastic happiness—princesses never complain.

Even when I'd rip one of their arms off. Always the same, perfect smile.

It's easy to wallow in despair. Knowing there's nothing worse. I make up these stories with no nuance, where all error and doubt have been erased. Gone is the tiring blur of the old days. I fight against pictures that are clear, and therefore true. I almost died. For a moment, that comforts me.

If I could scream louder, would I feel better? Red can be red like love, too. Matías emerges and asks me, Chloé, what do you want out of life? Ser feliz, I answer. He just stands there, not sure what to make of it.

I don't know what happened anymore. I think back and there's hardly anything left. Nothing that explains the gaps between the answers.

It's for you, you know. The package? I didn't even think to check.

You're not gonna open it? Emilio hands me the envelope from across the room, shakes it. A padded brown envelope. With a lot of stamps. A mischievous look on his face, Chloé, you have mail. How is that possible? Something over-whelming comes over me, a mix of too much of everything. I'm suddenly in another room far far away from here. Headrush, I need to sit down.

So? Him, up close, too close. My vision blurred. Who is it? No one.

I'm fiddling around with my fork in what's left of the spaghetti sauce on my plate. Emilio asks Adriana how her cupcake business is going—her latest venture. She's fluttering around the room. Would have loved to show him the sparkly bubblegum-pink icing she managed to make into a mushroom-cap shape. Where were you? You missed out on my masterpiece!

Adriana isn't wearing nail polish. It's weird, she looks naked. I'll make more for you, don't worry. Emilio gives only one-syllable answers. Doesn't seem very interested in what she's saying. Aggressive, even. If you didn't want to know, you didn't have to ask. What did Gloria do this time? Want me to talk to her? Look at the state she's got you in. He shakes his head. Abruptly changes the subject. Wow, you two really are a blast tonight. Great vibe, thanks guys. I'm not inviting you out, stay here and work on turning those frowns upside down. Emilio says he feels a flu coming on, shuts himself in his room.

Clowndog, Kloundog, Klog, Clawg. Conedog, Cog, Coggie? I'll come up with a name for you one of these days.

Don't be scared, Betty. It's a sun I'm drawing for you. Bright rays in the middle of your empty sky. Look how happy you look now. The paint marks the walls with my fingerprints. My prints, just mine. My thumb and four fingers stamped on the wall. If you're good, Betty, I'll draw stars for you too. I could fill the room with stars. What do you think? Do you think we'd have better dreams? I only have red, though, I hope that's okay. The red was on special.

On Emilio's desk, piles of paper, mostly scribbles and words that are crossed out. With arrows in the margins, illegible annotations. The next play? The same one? I sit down on his bed.

I lie down in it. It smells like him. And her a bit, too. He could show up at any moment. I shove my face into the pillows, fighting the odds. Deliciously illegal, in his bed. I roll around in the covers a little. And I start crying.

What do I do if he walks in? What do I say?

He has a spot on his wall too. I can see it, blurry through my soaked eyes. Maybe he wouldn't even be surprised to find me in his bed.

He'd lie down, I'd take his hand. You have nice hands, you know, I'd say.

I'd clear my throat and go on. A lot of lines, that's a good sign. Success in these curves. Some crosses, but nothing too bad. A long life line here, deep. Look, all full of—what would you like your life to be full of? My turn.

Do you know the lines of your palm? Look. This one's my life line. You see how it's all mixed up with my heart line?

QC FICTION

Current & Upcoming Books

Visit **qcfiction.com** for details and to subscribe
to a full season of QC Fiction titles.

MIX
Paper from
responsible sources
FSC® C100212
www.fsc.org

Printed by Imprimerie Gauvin
Gatineau, Québec